The Stranger at Winfield House

Wilma Yeo

AN
APPLE
PAPERBACK

SCHOLASTIC INC.
New York Toronto London Auckland Sydney

For Donald Williams
who makes all things possible
and for Marji and Don McDonald
and Marli and Buzz O'Brien

ISBN 0-590-43912-X

12 11 10 9 8 7 6 5 4 3   1 2 3/9

Printed in the U.S.A.   28

First Scholastic printing, September 1989

1

This spring my whole family got sliced into pieces like a sweet potato pie. My big brothers, Lance and Jim Joe, decided to stay on in Durham for the summer college classes. As if that wasn't bad enough, Dad left us. Only Dad left for good.

My dad had said to me one time, "Sisterbaby" (that's what he calls me even though my name is rightly Dorinda), "Sisterbaby," he said, "your mama's and my friendship is in bad trouble." Still I never even imagined my dad would truly leave us. But right after that, he did.

When he left, Mama said with tears in her voice, "Dorinda, honey, I reckon it's just you and me and Soon Gone now."

My dad was the one who gave my cat, Soon Gone, her name. Our preacher's wife had dropped her into my trick-or-treat sack on Halloween night two years ago. When my dad, who hates cats, saw her, he said, "It can stay here tonight, Sisterbaby, but that cat's going to be *soon gone*." Funny. I've kept that cat ever since, and now it's my father who is gone.

I missed my brothers and my dad something awful, but I didn't let on too much to Mama because she was carrying on sad enough for the both of us.

With school out for the summer, that made me the big problem. I tried to convince Mama that eleven was old enough to stay by myself while she was at the mill office working. Mama wouldn't agree to that.

"Honey," she said, laying her hand on my cheek, "what you really need is a grandma."

"Well, you can't just conjure up one of *those* out of swamp water and snake bellies," I reminded her. I was trying to make her laugh, but she raised her eyebrows and looked secretive. I was worried right then that Mama had another one of her famous "inspirations."

Turned out I was right to worry. What Mama had in mind was that the two of us would move to an apartment in the old Winfield House. The house is on the Winfield Plantation clear out to the edge and beyond of Charleston.

"Why, Dorinda, honey," Mama said, "that big old house out there is likely full of grandmas. A couple of grandpas, too, I reckon. You can just have your little old pick and choosin'.."

"No, ma'am," I yelled, "I plain can't spend my whole summer at that place. What would I do all day? I won't even know anyone clear off out there."

Mama got teary again. "I declare, I don't know what else to do. I talked with Miss Lizzie who owns Winfield House, and she will be just pleased to see to you a bit while I'm at work. There's an empty apartment we can have up on the third floor of the big house. And Dorinda, there's a boy your age living in the house, too."

It sure wasn't the part about the boy made me say, "Well, okay. We can try it I guess." It was Mama's tears made me say it.

The next Saturday Mama and I drove in our beat-up station wagon out to Miss Lizzie's plantation house, which is still called the old Winfield House, on Croker Sack Road. Miss Lizzie is a black woman, and they say her grandpa was a slave who worked the tobacco beds and barns on

3

that same land back when Mr. Winfield, a white man, owned the plantation. Miss Lizzie had the house divided into apartments, mostly lived in by old people.

We parked in the front beside an old iron hitching post with a little horse's head on it. The big brick house had four huge columns on the front that needed painting. The yard was gone to sand and tufts of tobacco grass. I stumbled over an old iron foot scraper half hidden by the seedy grasses.

A faded Confederate flag hung sad-looking from a brown jug sitting on the cracked cement porch.

As Mama and I went through the wide door, she had her hand resting on the back of my neck. It felt like she was pushing me, but I knew my mama well enough to know she was really just steadying herself. It wasn't easy for either one of us to give up our own house and neighborhood.

Even though I knew Mama needed me to be strong, I said, "Mama, are you certain sure this is what we want to be doing?"

Mama just gave a little squeeze to the back of my neck and did not answer me.

Inside the front door there was an entry hall that was shut off from the rest of the house by a door with a stained-glass window which had bunches of grapes on it. On one wall was a great tall-backed seat that had an oval mirror with claw-like hooks all around. Hanging on one hook was a basket with a note pinned to it that said Mail.

We went through the door with the purple glass window and then we were inside another hall that was huge and didn't have any furniture or rugs. The back of my neck where Mama's hand had been felt cold. This was some kind of a spooky place all right — just as I had pictured it would be from seeing the outside. There was not a sound any-where, and I wondered if maybe all those old peo-ple living here had just up and died and nobody even noticed.

"Let's try this door, honey," Mama whispered, motioning to the closest one. I heard her take a deep breath, and I knew she was most likely thinking the same as I was — that she wished we could get gone from this place and stay gone.

Mama knocked and before long the door opened slowly, and one brown eye and part of a nose and mouth showed. I supposed it was Miss Lizzie.

When the eye saw it was Mama and me, the door opened wider. "You all come right along in," the lady said, peering over our shoulders as if she wanted to make sure nobody else saw us. It was

Miss Lizzie all right. I wondered what she was so scared of right here in her very own house.

Miss Lizzie must be a hundred years old, I thought. She led Mama and me into a big high-ceilinged room that smelled like collards cooking. The front part was her sitting room. There was a davenport with an afghan on it and two big flowered chairs with a yellow cat curled asleep in one of them. Farther back in the room was a china cupboard and a table and chairs.

As Miss Lizzie handed Mama the keys to the third floor apartment, so we could see about it, she said, "You all will have to go on up alone. These old knees won't set with me climbing steps anymore."

Then, just as we were part way out her door she whispered, "Only one other person living up there on the third floor. That's Mr. Skeehan." She looked toward the wide stairway at the back of the hall, then slowly looked up the stairs and added like a warning, "Mr. Skeehan, he sleeps days." She nodded as if she was agreeing with herself.

I wanted to ask what Mr. Skeehan did nights! This was one spooky place all right.

As soon as Mama and I were outside Miss Lizzie's apartment door, I heard the key turn in the lock behind us. I wondered again what she was so scared of. Was she afraid of Mr. Skeehan who lived on the very same floor we might be living on?

As Mama and I went toward the wide stairway leading to the second floor I heard a door squeaking slowly open above us. The plain born truth, I warned myself, is that this old house is some kind of a nut house and come a week from Monday morning, I'm likely to be stuck here alone all day every day. At least I'd have my cat.

Mama looked at me, so I put on a smile that slid right back off when she looked away again, and we started up the second flight of stairs. These steps were so narrow Mama and I had to walk single file. The higher we went the hotter it got until in the third floor hallway you could pure *smell* the heat.

At the top of the steps we came to a closed door that had a little card held onto it with one red and one blue thumbtack. Someone had written on the card in spidery looking letters, A Southern Patriot Lives Here. That Mr. Skeehan really is weird, I thought, shrugging off a shiver which I hoped Mama hadn't noticed.

7

I knew Mama was plain shaky about this as I was. She crossed the hall and unlocked the door to the empty apartment. "I declare, it's not bad at all, Dorinda, honey," she said, pushing the door all the way open.

In front of us was what I s'posed was the living room. The two windows were narrow and went all the way to the floor. I walked over to look out. Twisting down from one window was a black iron fire escape that reached all the way to the ground.

Besides that room, there were three little bedrooms. The one Mama said would be mine had pink roses on the wallpaper, and the ceiling sloped on one side. It smelled like an attic, but it was cozy. There was a kitchen and a tiny bathroom with a rust-streaked tub set up off the floor on claw feet.

"Why sure, Mama," I said, "it's gonna be just fine." I felt the inside of my forehead tickle like it does when I tell a lie. The truth was that nothing was ever going to be just fine again.

For the next week, nothing made me change my mind. I stayed right alongside Mama helping her pack up our things. If I so much as left long enough to let Soon Gone in or out our door, I'd like as not come back to find Mama sitting on a packing box with her hands over her face.

I guess the saddest part of all was when we boxed up Lance and Jim Joe's things. As I dropped Jim Joe's ball glove into the box, I could almost hear him saying, "Hey, catch this one, kid."

Finally everything was packed. The next morning, moving men came and loaded everything onto their truck. Mama, my cat, Soon Gone, and I drove ahead of the truck on out Croker Sack Road to Winfield House.

Mama already had the key to our apartment, and we went all the way up to the third floor without seeing a soul. And like before, we heard doors creak open behind us. Even though I had on jeans I tried to pretend I was a princess, and those doors opening were people peeking out to see a princess passing by.

Mama and I worked the rest of the day getting our things unpacked and set in place. We put Lance and Jim Joe's things in the big bedroom but didn't unpack the boxes. Soon Gone wandered around looking miserable as I felt.

About five o'clock we had just sat down to catch our breath and decide where to go get a sandwich when the phone rang.

Mama answered it. I could tell right off from watching her face it was Dad. Maybe, I thought, oh sweet lordy, maybe Dad wants to come home — or to what is home now, I added, looking around. I watched Mama's face real close while she talked. She didn't look happy, but she didn't look mad he'd called, either.

When Mama hung up she let her hands fall limp to her sides and said, "Dorinda, your father and I need to talk over some things. He asked me to meet him" — she walked over to one of the skinny windows and looked out — "but I can't take you along, and I hate leaving you here alone the very first night because — "

"But I won't be alone, Mama," I said almost too fast. I wanted more than anything for Mama and Dad to talk and maybe work things out so we could be a family again. "If Soon Gone hears you say that," I added, trying to make it sound like a joke, "she'll be insulted. And anyway, like you said, there's Miss Lizzie close as downstairs."

"That's sure enough right," Mama said, looking brighter. "And I'm not meeting your father until nine so you and I will just take our own sweet time and drive over to South Beach for some good food before I leave. And I swear I won't be gone long, honey."

Mama was determined to stop by Miss Lizzie's door on our way out to eat and tell her I'd be upstairs alone later on.

Miss Lizzie said, "Now that's going to be just fine, you hear?" Then she looked around the hall as if she wanted to make sure nobody else was around and added, "Mr. Skeehan won't be up there, of course. He leaves sharp at seven-thirty. Poor old fellow. Night watchman. At his age. Works seven nights of the week."

Mama said her thanks and we left. I couldn't help feeling better to find out what Mr. Skeehan did at night. Night watchman sounded safe as home base to me.

Turned out later I was wrong.

2

Mama and I had a nice supper at South Beach. The breeze blew in from the ocean, fresh as a drink of iced tea. But somehow the pelicans' cries outside the open window sounded like a warning.

It was early dark when Mama turned our station wagon back up the long lane leading to Winfield House. The lane was paved with crushed oyster shells, called tabby. To one side of the lane was a row of cabins sitting deserted-looking under some straggly pecan trees. Mama explained they were built long ago for slave quarters. I thought the poor little cabins looked sad and apologetic.

But the big house, rising up out of the piney woods looked almost elegant at night — like pictures of the way the plantations used to be long ago. You couldn't see the peeling paint on the high columns. The jasmine vines climbing the brick walls of the house were in bloom and smelled sweet as honey. And the great live oak trees dripped their lacy moss down like a blessing.

Inside the empty front hall there was a piddling bit of light coming from a dusty old chandelier with most of its flame-shaped bulbs burned out. As usual, Mama and I went up the wide steps without seeing anyone around. But on the second floor, you could hear voices — a man's and a woman's.

The man's voice sounded angry, even though we couldn't hear what he was saying. We could hardly hear the woman's voice at all. We hurried on up the stairs to the third floor.

It was almost nine o'clock, and I sure didn't want Mama to be late meeting my dad. I wanted everything to go as good as it could. Hearing those voices on the second floor made me think of how Mama and Dad used to talk way into the night.

"I'll be just fine now, Mama," I said, trying to hurry her along. "Soon Gone is glad I'm home, and we'll just watch TV cozied up here together."

After Mama told me for the fifth time to be sure and lock the door behind her, and to go straight down to Miss Lizzie's if I had any trouble at all, I said, "Hush your fussin', Mama. I'm going to be just fine."

She left and I wandered around the rooms a while, telling myself all the good things that could happen when Mama met my dad. Like whoever was to blame could say they were sorry.

Then I decided to turn on the television. Soon Gone hopped up onto the davenport beside me and stepped one foot after the other onto my lap. She curled her whole heavy self into a contented ball and went to sleep.

I had the sound turned low because, being alone, I felt like I had to keep one ear out for any strange noises. After a while I got clear into the story on the screen and forgot about listening to anything else.

That's when I heard it!

It sounded like heavy footsteps were coming up the third floor stairs!

I listened carefully. Clump thump clump, like clumsy Frankenstein footsteps coming slowly up the narrow stairway.

I told myself it could be rusty water pipes from one of the apartments below us. But I knew I was fooling myself. Somebody was climbing the steps.

But it was way too early for Mama to be coming back.

Maybe that Mr. Skeehan didn't work tonight after all, I thought as I eased Soon Gone off my lap. She twitched one ear the way she does when she feels cross at me. I tiptoed over to our door to listen.

Suddenly there was a sharp thud that for positive sure came from right outside our door. I *had* to see what was going on. The old lock made a noisy click when I turned it, and I almost lost my nerve. For a few seconds I just stood there trying not to breathe so loud.

Finally I pushed the door open a crack and peeked into the dim light of the hallway. Even in this creepy old house, I never expected to see what I saw.

Across the hall near the top of the stairs, the legs and feet of a man's body were being pulled right through Mr. Skeehan's doorway!

I jerked our door shut, careful at the last split second not to slam it for fear whoever was doing the pulling of the body would catch me spying on them. I locked the door and braced my back against it. All the time I was trying hard to make myself believe that whatever was going on in this house didn't have anything to do with Mama and me. Especially not if it was murder. And those feet pointing straight up sure hadn't looked much alive.

I thought about grabbing Soon Gone and taking out for Miss Lizzie's apartment. But I was too scared because of what might happen between where I *was* and where I'd have to get *to*. I didn't even want to unlock our door again.

I went back over to the davenport and scooped up Soon Gone who was peacefully sleeping. Just being close to something else alive made me feel better. I looked over at the windows. One was open and without any curtains up yet. The outside darkness seemed to melt right into the living room. I put Soon Gone down and went over to close the window. A foggy drizzle had shined the black iron fire escape, but blotted out everything beyond it.

I pushed on the top of the window to close it. At first it wouldn't move at all and then suddenly it slammed all the way to the bottom! I jumped back as if the noise had been a gunshot and looked over toward the front door. Everything was quiet except the murmuring sound coming from the television.

For a while I sat hunched on the davenport staring at the TV and not seeing a thing that was going on. You're borrowing trouble, I scolded at myself. My dad was always big on not borrowing trouble. He always said, "Every living person has plenty of his own trouble without borrowing any."

Maybe there is an everyday reasonable reason for what I saw in the hallway, I told myself. After all, Mr. Skeehan *is* a night watchman, so he can't be too awful. I squared my shoulders so I would at least *look* brave. That seemed to make things a tolerable bit better.

Then all at once I heard footsteps in the hallway! I squeezed Soon Gone so tight she let out a sharp "merrow" and jumped off my lap. I heard a key turn and the door opened. It was Mama.

I was so glad to see her, I almost started bawling like a little baby. I guess cats and mothers are the only two things you can count on for sure in the world, I thought as I hugged Mama good.

She looked tired and I knew nothing wonderful had happened when she met my dad. She had tears in her voice as she said, "Your father asked me to — to file for a divorce, Dorinda."

I started to hug her again, but she walked over to the window and said out into the darkness, "I told him I couldn't do it." She took a deep breath. "And he wants you to come visit him."

Right that minute I truly hated my dad for hurting Mama that way. "Well, I'm not going to go," I said. "Never ever." Mama didn't say anything to that. She just kissed me good night and went on into her own room.

I decided I wouldn't worry Mama by telling her anything about what went on in the hall that night while she was gone. But come morning, I vowed to myself, *some* way, I'm going to find out what's going on around here, so I can protect Mama and me both.

3

After I was in bed, I lay awake listening to the whispery night sounds of the swamp critters. I thought about how once my dad had told me that in the summer the swamps were the haunt of the coot and the hern. I wished I had asked him what those were.

Then to get my mind off Dad, and to keep it away from what I had seen in the hallway, I tried to tell some of the swamp critters' sounds apart. It was easy to tell the swamp frogs from the night hawk's shivering cries. I imagined an owl sitting on a cypress root giving those pitiable hoots.

It didn't work long though because pretty soon I was staring up at the slopey rain-stained ceiling of my new room and wondering what I would do all day while Mama was at work. And most of all

I wondered what was happening right across the hall at that very minute.

I guess I was sleepier than I thought because next I knew Mama was calling me to get up for breakfast. She was already dressed for work. I put on my jeans and my blue shirt with the extra long shirttail which I'd been saving for summer vacation.

By the time Mama finally left for work she had hugged me near about to pieces and given me a million instructions. She promised to listen to what happened in the library book I was reading when she got home, and to tell me all about her day. But I already had in mind what I was going to do instead of read. Once I cleared up our few breakfast dishes, I was going to do some exploring around the place.

Since it was daylight, and a sunny day top of that, I didn't feel nearly so uneasy about staying there alone. But I still couldn't get the thought out of my mind of those feet disappearing into the apartment across the hall.

I fed Soon Gone her favorite cat food and promised her I'd be back before long. Even though I wasn't really scared, I opened our door slowly and peeked out.

The only daylight in the third floor hall seeped through a shuttered window at the far end. The hall seemed almost as gloomy as it had last night. Mr. Skeehan's door was closed.

The stairway smelled like burned coffee and a mixture of strange breakfasts cooking. Just as I got to the bottom of the second, wider set of stairs, I heard a door slam and then pounding footsteps from above me. I glanced up and saw the grinning face of a boy about my age. I hurried on across the downstairs hall, hoping he wouldn't catch up to me. I had no mind to get acquainted with anyone in this stupid place.

But before I could even get the first door open, he skidded across the bare floor and opened it for me.

"G'mornin', m'lady," he said making a ridiculous bow as I breezed right straight past him.

"Name's Tilford Jones," he said, following me out the second door, which I had opened for myself. "But you may call me Tilford Short." When I ignored him and walked on across the porch he kept talking, "Get it? Til-for-short?"

I kept right on walking across the yard just like I knew where I was going. I headed for a giant chinaberry tree to one side of the yard.

"Want to see what I can do?" the boy asked, keeping right alongside me.

"Why should I?" I said, sounding stuck up as I could.

"Miss Lizzie told me your name," he said just as if I had been friendly. Then he ran a few steps ahead, leaped, landed on both hands and walked along with his head down and his taffy-colored hair dragging in the tobacco grass sprouting through the sand.

I could barely keep from laughing. At last he flipped forward and landed neat as a thistle on his feet in front of me. He spread his arms and bowed as if I had applauded. "I'm going to be a clown someday," he said, grinning.

"If you want my opinion, you already are," I said, mad at myself for almost laughing. I brushed past him and kept on walking even though I had already come to the chinaberry tree. Ahead of me were sand dunes sprouting some straggly sea oats.

"No, I really am," he said, catching up again. "My father is Happy."

"That you're going to be a clown?" I couldn't keep from asking.

"No, he *is* Happy."

"That's nice," I said, wondering how far he was going to follow me. I knew the swamps began beyond the dunes so I couldn't walk much farther. I decided to stop and just stand there and see what he would do.

"How about your father?" he asked. He had stopped now, too, and was facing me.

I truly surprised myself by blurting out, "If you must know, my father and Mama are going to get divorced, so I suppose you could say that he's happy, too — now."

Quickly as if he'd taken off one mask and put on another, Tilford Jones's funny face turned sad. "Gee, I'm sorry. See, my father really is Happy Jones, the clown. When we save enough money, he's going to Clown College. I meant what does your father do."

"Oh." I hated him for feeling sorry for me, and I still felt shaky inside because that was the first time I'd truly said the word *divorce* out loud. Maybe it would never happen. I wished desperately I could take it back. I turned and started walking slowly back toward Winfield House. Tilford Jones walked right along beside me, of course.

"Clowning is serious business," Tilford said as

if he was eager to make me believe he was something more than a show-off. "Clown College is in Venice. That's in Florida."

"I *know*," I said, but of course I didn't on account of why should I?

"Anyway," he said, "I'm glad you moved to Winfield House, Dorinda Saunders. It'll be almost like there's another kid in my family." And then, like he was scared he'd said too much, he raced on ahead of me with his shirttail flying behind him. He jumped the two front steps, landed on the porch and disappeared inside the big house.

I thought about what he had said. *Me* a part of his family? Never! I have my own family, I thought, even if three of them *are* missing. Even if it is only Mama and me right at this present time. I sat down on the bottom step leading to the porch and looked over where the huge live oaks huddled like tired giants with their gnarled limb-arms clutching at one another and the Spanish moss dripping down off them like frizzled hair.

That old man across the hall isn't the only weird person living in this house, I told myself. I sat there hating to go back upstairs, but not knowing what else to do with myself. I tried to think of a plan for solving the mystery of Mr. Peter Skee-han.

Sometimes good ideas come to me when I'm riding my bike. I decided to go for a bike ride and pretend I was a detective.

My bike was parked under the goldenrain tree by the carport at the back of the house. Miss Lizzie had told Mama she could park our station wagon there, so we figured it was right for my bike to be there, too. The only other cars back there were Miss Lizzie's rattle-trap pickup, which she told us she used to carry groceries to some of the folks who lived here, and a rusted jeep.

I picked a cluster of sticky pink pods that had fallen from the goldenrain tree out of my basket and wheeled my bike around to the tabby lane.

I stopped there with only one foot on a pedal because I noticed a car parked about halfway down the lane. I could see there was a man sitting in the driver's seat. The car looked new — or at least new for around here. Around here the salty ocean air fades paint on cars so fast that you don't rightly see many new-looking ones.

I had thought about riding up Croker Sack Road past Creepin' Charlie Swamp, but my one foot seemed to be stuck there to the ground.

No cause to be scared, I scolded myself. Sitting there is no crime. I hopped onto my bike. But as I got closer I hunched over and pedaled hard to hurry past the man in the car. He had a pale skinny face and was wearing one earring. I could feel his eyes on my back even after I was a ways down the lane.

My ride was purely ruined. My legs felt too weak to pedal me all the way to Gallberry Brush Beach which Mama had explained was just a half mile beyond the swamp. What if that man followed me? What was he doing parked halfway down our lane anyway?

When I'd only gone as far as the swamp I turned around and headed back. Even though I'd have to go past that man again, I felt like I had to get back home. I told myself I was just spooked out because of what had happened last night. But I felt like everything was closing me into a smaller and smaller space.

I breathed better when I came back to the start of our lane and saw that the parked car was gone. Probably just a magazine salesman getting up courage to go on up to the big house, I scolded myself. Don't be such a coward.

When I came even with the little cabins Mama had said used to be slave quarters, I decided to prove I wasn't really scared by stopping to explore them.

The four one-room cabins, made of old bricks held together with crumbling cement, stood in a forlorn row. Each one had a doorway but no door. I stepped up into the first of the little buildings. There was a high square window on each side of the room and a spider webby hole of a fireplace in the middle of the back wall.

I tried to pretend I was a slave girl living here. Right away I wondered where they took a bath or where they went to the bathroom. I wondered if Miss Lizzie's grandpa had lived in one of the tiny houses with his wife and children. Maybe even Miss Lizzie herself. Did she ever come down here and look inside the quarters where black people once lived as slaves? If she did, what did she think about? It seemed hard to believe that any American people were really slaves of other American people.

Suddenly I heard footsteps in the dry johnson grass outside the cabin. Thinking of the man in the lane, I whirled toward the door opening. I sure didn't want to be trapped inside!

4

It was only Tilford Jones! He was tossing a ball of string in the air and catching it behind his back as he waded through the tall grass. I started breathing again.

"Dad and I save this stuff," Tilford said, holding the string ball out for me to see. "Dad has a real class act he does with it. The string unwinds behind him, see? But he pretends he doesn't notice. All the time this other clown, a joey, is following Dad and rewinding it into a ball of his own. It's funny when he does it. You'll see."

I wondered if Tilford Jones ever thought about anything except clowning and his father. "I declare if I will," I said. "And I wish you'd stop following me around."

Tilford Jones just smiled and wiggled his ears

at me. "It's right hard to say it with you acting this way, but I meant what I said yonder — about being glad you and your Mama moved here."

"I hate living out here on this spooky old plantation," I said. "I'm sure that when my mama gets a raise at the mill office, we'll be moving back where we lived before."

"Well, until then I'm right proud to know you," Tilford said smooth as buttered grits. But at least he had stopped grinning at me. "Living out here is almost like living with a bunch of grandparents," Tilford went on. I thought about what Mama had said before we moved here.

"Even that crazy old man who lives on the third floor with us?" I asked. "Some kind of grandfather he is!"

"He's okay," Tilford said, looking at me in a puzzled way. "Sort of odd, I reckon. But he's not crazy. I call him Mr. Peter Skeeter because with those thick glasses and his little bald head, he looks like a mosquito."

With his hands on his head Tilford Jones did an imitation of an old man bent over and peering blindly out of buggy-looking eyes. "I sort of like him," he added, looking pleased with himself.

"He is crazy," I said, "and probably a criminal."

I wondered if I'd be sorry for telling him all this.

"Naw," Tilford Jones said, "Mr. Peter Skeeter's no criminal. He's a night watchman. He's even a deputy sheriff. Got a badge to prove it. He puts that old Confederate flag out every morning when he comes home from work and takes it down every night when he goes out. He's just a harmless old man who still thinks the South will rise again. Least that's what my dad says."

"Shows how much your dad knows," I said. I wondered if Tilford would accuse me of making it up if I told him what I'd seen in Mr. "Peter Skeeter's" doorway last night.

"My dad knows plenty," Tilford said. He narrowed his eyes at me, and right away I was sorry I'd said that about his dad, so I just plain blurted out the whole story of what I'd seen in the hallway.

When I came to the part about the shoes disappearing through Mr. Skeehan's doorway, Tilford shook his head as if he couldn't believe it. He seemed to be so concerned now that I finished up by admitting, "It scared me plumb cold!"

"You say you didn't really see either person? The one dragging or the one being dragged —

just his feet?" Tilford's forehead was a mess of wrinkles.

I nodded.

"Then maybe it was Mr. Peter Skeeter *being* dragged!" Tilford exclaimed.

"Does he wear black and white shoes — new looking?" I asked. Truth was I was grateful that Tilford hadn't laughed or made fun of me for admitting I was scared the way most boys would have.

"Doesn't sound like him," Tilford said, running his hand through his straight taffy-colored hair. "You say this was about nine-thirty? I wonder why he wasn't at work at the department store. He goes to his night watchman's job at seven-thirty every night. Maybe it was two other people you saw. I think we should get ourselves up there and see if the old fellow is okay."

"You mean just knock on his door?" I asked. "But what will you say?"

Tilford pretended to pull off an invisible hat and hold it over his heart. "Hello. Nice day. Anything I can do for you? Carry out any trash? Sweep out any dead bodies?"

This time I didn't try to keep from laughing. I

had never seen anyone who could put on as many faces as Tilford Jones could. But suddenly a scary thought came to me. "I don't want him knowing who told you," I said.

"Don't worry," Tilford said. "You'll come with me, won't you?"

"I declare if I will!" I said. "I don't know anything about that old man, and what's more I don't want to know anything. Badge or no badge!"

"Oh, well, that's okay," Tilford said, looking at me kind of funny again. "I reckon I'd best get myself on up there." He turned and started toward the big house.

I waited until he was almost to the steps of the plantation house, then I followed him. I had promised myself I'd find out what was going on, and I saw my chance.

5

By the time I got inside the front hall, Tilford was out of sight. I crept up the wide set of steps to the second floor and tiptoed over to the bottom of the third floor steps. Tilford was almost to the top of that stairway. I had planned to wait at the bottom step and listen to what went on between Tilford Jones and Mr. Skeehan, but suddenly Tilford began acting really strange.

At first I thought he had caught on I had followed him and was putting on an act for me. He leaned down and sort of sniffed his way along for a couple of steps then crashed on up and began beating on Mr. Skeehan's door and yelling his name. Then he tried the doorknob but it was locked. He looked around wild-eyed and saw me gawking up at him. I had forgotten all about keeping hidden. Something must be terribly wrong!

"Quick, Dorinda, help me. Gas!" he yelled down.

"I'll get help," I shouted, turning to run.

But Tilford yelled, "No time! Here!"

I dashed on up the steps and even before I got to the top, Tilford began shouting orders. "The roof — under your kitchen window — goes clear around — fast!"

As we ran toward our apartment door I fished in my jeans pocket for the key. My hand shook as I pushed the key into the lock. What about Soon Gone! What if the whole house blew up. At least the smell of gas wasn't so strong by our doorway.

While Tilford raised our kitchen window I shoved Soon Gone into Mom's bedroom and shut the door. Just before I crawled through the open window after Tilford, I grabbed Mom's heavy iron skillet I'd washed up after breakfast and carried it along through the window with me.

"Good thinking," Tilford breathed as he pulled me on through the window. "His window may be locked."

The tin roof, edged by a low spiky railing, popped and creaked under our feet as we hurried toward Mr. Skeehan's window. I looked down and saw a woman watching us from the yard far below.

"Hey, Mrs. Potts," Tilford yelled down at her,

"Trouble in Mr. Skeehan's place. Get help."

But before he got all that said, the woman had scurried out of sight like a scared mole.

Mr. Skeehan's window was closed, but through the flimsy curtain I saw a man slumped over in a big easy chair.

"Push!" Tilford commanded, spreading his feet apart and shoving up on the window frame. I let go of the skillet and added all my strength to the other side of the window. It creaked lose a tiny bit.

"Again!" Tilford cried. This time the inside lock must have broken loose because the window slammed all the way to the top. We pushed the curtains out of our way and both of us tried to climb in at the same time.

But before our feet touched the floor inside, a man's voice demanded, "Get out or I'll shoot!"

For a second neither Tilford nor I moved. Then we both scrambled to get off that windowsill at once. We landed back out on the tin roof in a tangle of arms and legs. Before we could even get on our feet to run back to my window the deep voice came again, "Get out or I'll shoot."

This time I got suspicious. "Listen," I whispered, grabbing Tilford's arm. We ducked down listening as the voice repeated the same words in exactly the same tone.

Tilford and I looked at each other. Then like we could read each other's minds we got slowly to our knees to peek over the edge of the windowsill.

I stared in the direction the mechanical-sounding voice was still coming from. Standing in one corner of the room was a department store mannequin! The voice was coming right out of it. The mannequin was wearing old pants and a shirt, both too small for him. But on his feet were a shiny new pair of shoes — black and white shoes. The same shoes I had seen being dragged into Mr. Skeehan's apartment the night before.

I swished the curtain back for a better look. The heavy smell of gas near-about choked me, but I saw that the mannequin wasn't even holding a gun. The recorder inside the mannequin had hushed now. I heard Tilford yell, "Mr. Skeehan, sir!" as he hurled himself through the window ahead of me.

By the time I had climbed inside, Tilford was bending over the old man shaking him. Gas was pouring into the room. I saw that a pan of turnip greens on the stove had boiled over and put out the flame. I rushed to the stove and turned the gas off.

Even though we were coughing and choking something awful we managed to drag him out of the apartment into the hallway.

He still hadn't moved on his own, so I laid my head on his chest to listen and see if he was breathing.

"Is he dead?" Tilford whispered in a scared voice.

6

Just as Tilford said "dead" Mr. Skeehan moaned. I jumped back so fast I near about toppled over because he opened two of the most fierce-looking eyes I ever did see.

There was something really strange about his eyes. He's crazy just like I thought, I told myself. I was for getting out of there as quick as possible. But my knees were so weak they wouldn't lift me up off the floor. I looked across Mr. Skeehan at Tilford. "What — " I started to say, but Tilford interrupted me.

"Thank goodness you're all right, sir," he began, leaning down close to Mr. Skeehan's face. "We broke into your apartment because — "

"You — you broke into my apartment! The law — " Mr. Skeehan managed to get out before he began coughing again as he struggled to sit up.

I scooted myself back a ways farther down the hall.

"Sir, you don't understand," Tilford said, taking hold of Mr. Skeehan's arm to help him up. "Your mind is foggy from all that gas."

"Don't you go telling me about my mind, you whippersnapper," Mr. Skeehan cried.

I looked at Tilford. He shrugged. Then he leaned closer to Mr. Skeehan and said, "Do you recognize me, Mr. Skeehan, sir? Tilford Jones, remember?"

"Tilford? Tilford." Mr. Skeehan said the last word with relief in his voice. "What happened? Where am I?" He began feeling around on the floor beside him. "My glasses! What happened to my glasses?"

"Sir," Tilford said, "you fell asleep in your chair. Something boiled over on the stove and put out the flame."

"You're out in the hallway," I added. I felt right sorry for the poor old man. "Your glasses must be inside."

"Now who is that?" Mr. Skeehan asked, pointing his skinny, crooked finger at me.

"Oh, sir," Tilford said, "let me introduce you to this fine young lady. Her name is Miss Dorinda

Saunders. She has taken up residence across the hall yonder in order to go about Winfield House helping other people." Then he stopped clowning and added, "You can trust her, sir."

"Ever since someone stole my letter," Mr. Skeehan said, "I haven't been able to trust anyone, Tilford."

I wondered if Tilford actually believed this weird old man. Why would anyone want to steal a letter?

Mr. Skeehan stretched his neck like a turtle and looked around carefully before he whispered, "If they find out I can't do a good job protecting my own property, they will think I can't protect anyone else's." He shook his head. "I'll lose my job for sure."

Right at that moment I heard a creaking on the stairs behind us. I turned to look and caught a blurry glimpse of a woman's face peeking over the top step before the face disappeared. It was the same woman I had seen down below us in the yard when Tilford and I were on the roof. Mrs. Potts, Tilford had called her. Snoopy old woman, I thought. No wonder Mr. Skeehan is afraid of being overheard.

I looked at Tilford, but he was too busy helping

Mr. Skeehan to his feet to hear the woman as she creaked slowly down the third floor steps.

"Help me get him back into his own place, Dorinda," Tilford said. "Gas should be gone by now."

I was half scared about what he'd do, but I took hold of Mr. Skeehan's other arm like Tilford said, and we steered him toward his own doorway. The open door and window had cleared most of the gas smell out. Tilford and I walked the old man past the rigged-up mannequin and over toward a kitchen chair. Tilford picked up a pair of wire-rimmed glasses and handed them to him.

Mr. Skeehan put the glasses on and turned toward the mannequin, which was silent now. We all stared at it.

"I brought that fool thing home from the store where I work to scare off anybody else who got the idea to break in here," Mr. Skeehan explained. "But," he said, looking at us, "I guess it didn't work."

"It sure scared *me*," I said.

"Me, too," Tilford said. "But we were too worried about you to run off."

"Well, I guess the cat's out of the bag now." Mr. Skeehan sank into the chair as if his knees wouldn't hold him up a second longer.

"I will have to trust you two. Like I was saying, I can't go to the police. You see, I planned to sell my letter that was stolen and use the money to have my eye operation. I would lose my badge for sure if anyone knew how bad my eyes are. Ha! A watchman who can't even watch!" He shook his head, and a tear slid down a line on his cheek.

"I wasn't going to sell my letter, which is worth a lot of money, to just anyone," Mr. Skeehan went on. "I was going to make certain it went to a museum where it belonged."

I wondered what kind of letter could be so important.

"Maybe you only misplaced the letter, sir," Tilford said, putting his hand on Mr. Skeehan's shoulder. "Maybe we could help you find it."

"No siree, young man." Mr. Skeehan held up his hand palm out. "That letter was never misplaced. You see that book on the table there?"

I was standing next to the table and I touched a tall, narrow book made out of worn brown leather. "This book?" I asked.

"That's it," he said. "It's an old Civil War journal kept by my grandmother. Found it in her trunk over there after she died." He pointed to a black trunk with a rounded top in the far corner.

"Inside the journal's where I found the letter." He rubbed his hand across his eyes. "But now it's gone — stolen, like I said — while I was at work. I know I locked my door before I left. It was still locked the next morning when I got home from work. But who'd ever believe that now? There's just no way to figure it."

I touched the leather bound book. The cover was designed with different size squares marked off with gold. But the gold was mostly worn away. There was a dark circle on the brown leather, like someone long ago had set a wet glass on the book and left it there a long time.

"Who was your letter from?" Tilford asked Mr. Skeehan.

"That letter was written to my grandmother by Mr. Abraham Lincoln himself on the occasion of the death of my grandfather in the Civil War." Mr. Skeehan's voice cracked to a stop. Then he added hurriedly, "On the side of the glorious South, of course."

It was hard not to believe him.

He went on in that same crackly voice, "The letter said how Mr. Lincoln somewhat understood — having lost a son to death. Little Todd Lincoln."

"I'll help you find your letter, sir," Tilford said. He had that same sorry look on his face he got when I said my folks were going to get a divorce.

Mr. Skeehan just shook his head and looked at the floor. "You all better get on along now," he said. "Your folks will be wondering themselves purely to death over you. But first swear by the almighty South you won't tell a soul I was robbed."

Mentioning our folks made me think of Mama's skillet still out there on the roof. I wondered if I dared ask if we could leave through the window. I decided against asking because I certain sure didn't want to remind Mr. Skeehan that we had broken in through that window — that his funny old mannequin didn't even fool us.

Still if I didn't get the skillet Mama would likely ask about it. There was no way I could tell her the whole story short of setting her to fretting about me here alone, all over again.

Before I could decide what to do, Mr. Skeehan was closing his window and Tilford was saying good-bye and heading for the door. I wanted to ask Mr. Skeehan if anyone else knew about his Lincoln letter before it was stolen, but I couldn't make myself say it.

"I have to go see about my cat," I told Tilford when we were out in the hall again. What I really needed was to be by myself and think. So much had happened in the short time we'd been living in Winfield House it set my mind to spinning.

"Do you really believe him — about the letter, I mean?" I whispered to Tilford.

"Of course I believe him," Tilford said, wrinkling his forehead until it looked like lined paper. "But whether you do or not, Dorinda, you and I saved his life. That means we're responsible for him from now on." He grinned and dashed off down the third floor steps.

I headed for my own door. Everyone living in this house, *including* Tilford Jones, is weird as one of those characters in Alice in Wonderland, I decided.

7

Soon Gone was so mad at being locked in Mama's bedroom that she twitched her whiskers at me when I opened the door a crack to make sure she was okay. "I'll be right back," I promised, closing the door again. I still had to get Mama's skillet off the roof.

I figured I'd just hunch down and reach for the skillet and scuttle back to my own window. I checked the clock and it was still almost one hour before Mama would get home from work.

I was inching my way along as quietly as possible on the crackly tin roof when I heard a car coming up the lane leading to Winfield House. I scooched myself down best I could out of sight and peeked to make sure it wasn't Mama coming home early. She'd for sure want to know what I was doing up here.

If I told her somebody around here was breaking into people's apartments and stealing things, Mama would worry up a storm.

Anyway Tilford Jones and I had sworn to Mr. Skeehan that we wouldn't tell a soul about his robbery. I wasn't sure if that included even our parents, but between us swearing and Mama worrying, I knew I'd never tell.

The car stopped. It was the shiny one I'd seen parked halfway up our lane this morning! What was that man doing spying on our house this way?

I stayed frozen to the spot, hoping the skinny-faced man wouldn't notice me. Something about him made me shivery to my ankles. Before long I heard his motor start and when I looked up, I saw he was turning his car around.

I was sure he hadn't seen me. Soon as his car was out of sight I inched myself on until I could reach Mama's skillet. Dragging it along I crawled fast as I could move back to our own window and climbed inside.

Once the window was shut again and Soon Gone turned loose, I noticed what a mess my jeans and the palms of my hands were from the rust and dirt on the roof. I washed my hands good, but I knew Mama would notice if I should change to different clothes. I thought about telling her the whole story. Now that I wasn't scared of Mr. Skeehan, the mannequin part seemed really funny. Mama needed something to laugh about in her life. Far as that went, I myself would be glad to hear her laugh again like she used to.

But there was no way to tell without giving away Mr. Skeehan's secret, so I decided not to even begin.

I heard Mama's key in the lock, then I heard her call out, "Hey, Dorinda, honey, I'm home." I shoved all the bad part of the day clear to the back of my mind.

Mama and I fixed our supper together, and I told her about meeting Tilford Jones and about exploring the old slave cabins. Mama said we should be grateful to live in such a historic old place. "Is Tilford Jones nice?" Mama asked as she dished up the cornpones from the very skillet that had been on the roof. I guess that's the kind of question parents always ask their kids.

I thought about it for a second. *Nice* didn't somehow seem to fit Tilford Jones. "I reckon," I said with a little shrug. "He wants to be a clown when he grows up."

Mama laughed her pretty golden laugh. It made

me get a happy chill on the tops of my arms. "He'll change his mind 'bout that between now and when he's grown," she said.

I didn't say so, but I was mighty sure he wouldn't change his mind. It seemed so good to have Mama acting happy, even if it was only for a little while.

While we were still doing dishes Lance and Jim Joe called long distance to make sure Mama and I got moved in all right. Mama let me talk, too, of course, and for a while we almost seemed like a family again.

That night after we went to bed I had a hard time going to sleep. So much had gone on that I needed to think about. Maybe Tilford Jones and I really could help Mr. Skeehan find out who stole his Abraham Lincoln letter.

I guess it was because I laid awake so long thinking, that I overslept the next morning. I was having a dream that my dad was home in our old house. I woke up feeling cross. When I came into the kitchen, Mama was already dressed for work and my breakfast was warm on the stove. I was still wearing my shorty pajamas.

"I simply couldn't bear to wake you up, Sister-baby," Mama said, giving me a big hug, "but now I'm going to have to hurry off and leave you to eat by yourself." I wanted to yell, Don't call me Sisterbaby! Don't try to take my dad's place. I don't need him. I never want to see him again!

I didn't say it, of course. I just said, "Mornin' Mama. You sure do look pretty in that yellow dress."

Mama *is* pretty and now she had no one but me to tell her so. Used to be my brother Jim Joe would say to Mama, "You mighty good lookin', lady." Then he'd look at me and say, "And you, kid, are goin' be a real heartbreaker one of these days."

Now Mama and I are okay all by ourselves, I thought. And someday the boys will be with us again.

Mama finally left after fussing around about leaving me same as she had the morning before.

I had only swallowed about two bites of my egg and grits when I heard the key turn in our front door and Mama burst back into our apartment.

"I declare, Dorinda Saunders," Mama said, upset as all get out, "will you just please tell me what you and that boy were doing out on the roof yesterday?"

I was so surprised I couldn't say a word for a second. Finally I got out, "Yes, ma'am, how did you know?"

"One of the ladies who lives on the second floor saw you. She told me you were snooping around where you didn't belong. But that's not the thing, Dorinda," Mama said. "Don't you realize you could have fallen off the roof and been killed!"

I knew well and good it was *that* Mrs. Potts who told. Seeing Mama so upset again, I just knew for certain sure there was no way I was going to tell her the whole truth. "There *is* a railing, Mama," I said in a positive voice, "and it just looked fun."

The last part wasn't true, of course. My forehead began to tickle the way it always does when I tell a lie.

"Well, promise you won't do it again," Mama said. "I absolutely have to go along now. *Please* promise me, honey."

"Sure, I promise, Mama," I said. Sometimes I felt like I was the grown up and Mama the child. But nothing would have made me go out on that roof again once I'd made Mama that solemn promise.

But there was one thing I was sure positive about: I didn't go to make an enemy out of that Mrs. Potts, but if she kept snooping around in my life, I'd be her enemy forever!

8

Mama finally got on her way. I put on clean jeans and an old T-shirt my brother Lance gave me that said Duke University on it. I was finishing up the breakfast dishes when I heard a knock on the door. It was Tilford.

"Want to help?" he asked. "It's Friday, and Fridays I pick up people's trash and take it out back to burn."

"Sure," I said. Then remembering what had Mama so upset earlier I added, "All except that Mrs. Potts's trash. That snoopy tattle-taler can carry out her own trash for all I care."

Tilford sort of shrugged, but didn't say anything. It made me feel like I should apologize, but I couldn't think why.

I picked up our trash sack, and as we headed for Mr. Skeehan's door I told Tilford about Mrs.

Potts sneaking up the steps and watching us with Mr. Skeehan yesterday.

Tilford just shrugged again. But then he said, "My dad says Mrs. Potts is probably grouchy because she doesn't feel good. But I think maybe she's worried about something. Maybe just being old and alone. Miss Lizzie says Mrs. Potts has a son somewhere, but nobody around here has ever seen him."

Tilford knocked on Mr. Skeehan's door. In a few minutes he came and opened the door already carrying a green plastic trash basket. "Morning, y'all," he said sort of sadly.

He looked plumb worn out. I wondered if the gas had maybe made him sicker than we thought. Here I am worrying about him, I fussed at myself, when just yesterday I thought he was a murderer. I guess Tilford's right, I decided, when you help save someone's life you begin to feel responsible for them.

Mr. Skeehan looked around carefully and said, "I'm much obliged to the both of you — for everything."

"That's okay, sir," Tilford said, and I sort of smiled.

We went on down to the second floor. I held

Mr. Skeehan's trash basket while Tilford knocked on one of the other three doors besides his own. There was a small brass plate on the door that said Miss Katherine Eggerstead.

While we waited for the door to open, Tilford explained, "This is Miss Kate's place. She used to be a school teacher."

Miss Kate walked with a limp and had dyed black hair. She looked at Tilford and me as if she thought we were her pupils, and she had caught us in the wrong place at the wrong time. "Oh, it's you now," she said in a please-take-your-seats-and-be-quiet voice, "and what is it you want?" Her head shook a little bit as she talked.

"Miss Kate," Tilford said, making his mock bow and grinning at her. "Remember. It is Friday. The trash — may I once again have the honor?"

Miss Kate made her lips into a tighter line than they already were and left the doorway. In just a little bit she came back holding a large yellow can lined with a paper sack. "Mind you don't spill any of it," she said. But there was a tiny ghost of a smile on her lips as she snapped the door shut.

I looked at Tilford. It seemed like he and this Miss Kate were playing a game. But he just shrugged like always and said, "This next is Mr.

Digsby and I might as well warn you, he's sort of odd."

I just sighed.

That next door opened almost before Tilford had finished knocking. Mr. Digsby was short and fat and bald. He simply stood there looking at us with a vanilla pudding smile on his round face.

"I've come to carry out your trash," Tilford said softly.

"Well — " Mr. Digsby hesitated as if trusting us with his trash or not was a big decision. "I guess that would mean I wouldn't have to go down there," he finally said. "Now don't you go looking to see what's in it."

"That's right," Tilford said gently as if he were talking to a baby.

Mr. Digsby disappeared, and the door glided shut without a sound. I looked at Tilford not sure whether we were supposed to wait or not. But just then the door opened silently and a waste basket slid out onto the hall floor. "Be right sure it is all burned good," Mr. Digsby worried aloud from behind the almost closed door.

Tilford was right about one thing. Mr. Digsby was certainly strange. I decided this was going to be the weirdest summer of my life — emptying trash for a house full of crazy old people.

Tilford explained that the door across from Mr. Digsby's and directly below ours was Mrs. Potts's. "That's her trash already sitting out," he said. "She doesn't like to be bothered with me knocking."

I made a face at Mrs. Potts's closed door. We had all we could carry so Tilford said he'd come back for hers. We took the baskets on down to the first floor, out the back door at the end of the big hall and down two steps. The burner sat back under a huge live oak. The metal barrel had blackened a circle of ground around it. The circle was littered with old rusty wire hangers and half-burned paper.

We set the trash down and headed inside to get Mrs. Potts's basket and Miss Lizzie's on the first floor. Tilford explained that the rooms next to Miss Lizzie's, which used to be the library and dining room, had been empty as long as he had lived here.

"Miss Lizzie told me once she was saving those rooms for her black angels," Tilford said. "When I asked her when they were going to move in — those angels, I meant — she just laughed and said 'Any day now, boy. Just you be patient —

56

you gonna see. Yes, you gonna see.' "

Angels, I thought, living in empty rooms! Even Miss Lizzie, who was supposed to look after me, must be tetched. I didn't say anything to Tilford, though, because he already thought I was mighty thin-hided about these old folks he called his friends. And truth was, I was at least sort of getting to like Mr. Skeehan myself.

When we got back to the trash burner the wind had blown one of the baskets over. So, minding what Mr. Digsby had said, I began picking up the stray papers while Tilford dumped the other containers.

A small square card fluttered down and landed in front of me. As I picked that up, too, I noticed it had a little bunch of flowers painted on one side and the word Florist. There was no name on it, and I wondered who would have gotten flowers sent to them from a florist. Feeling a little guilty because of Mr. Digsby, I tossed the little card quickly into the barrel and picked up my share of the empties.

I took Mr. Skeehan's basket up to third. Tilford and I had agreed that when we finished we'd ride bikes over to Gallberry Brush Beach.

On my way up the narrow third floor steps I

tried to think of something friendly sounding to say to Mr. Skeehan. I decided to ask a polite question about his missing letter.

I almost lost my courage while I waited for him to answer my knock. But when he opened the door he was such a sorry-looking sight that I just had to try to cheer him up.

"Mr. Skeehan, sir," I said as I handed him his empty plastic basket, "Tilford and I will be right proud to help you, but we'll need some clues so as to" — I stopped and looked over my shoulder to be sure that snoopy Mrs. Potts wasn't lurking around somewhere — "help you find your you-know-what."

Mr. Skeehan motioned me to step inside so I figured he wanted to talk some more right then about his missing letter. When the door was safely closed and even locked behind us, I said, "Are you sure you recall locking your door the night your letter disappeared?"

"See here, missy," Mr. Peter Skeeter said, "it's my eyes that are bad — not my mind. My door was locked and I was away at work like always." He peered sharply at me through his thick eyeglasses. "It wasn't my fault they broke in, but nobody would understand that!"

I was beginning to wish Tilford was there. He'd know what to say next. Tilford Jones never seemed to run out of things to say.

"Did — did anybody besides you know about the letter?" I asked him, stalling until I could think of a better question.

"Nobody except the President," he said.

"The — the president of what?" I stammered. I sure was hoping he wouldn't say the President of the United States. It was right hard to think that Mr. Skeehan, who I was really beginning to like, was not right in the head after all. But that was exactly what he said!

"The President of the United States, of course, young missy," he said, looking pleased.

I felt a trickle of sweat run down between my shoulder blades. Maybe Mr. Peter Skeeter was crazy after all.

9

I glanced toward the locked door. I suddenly wondered what I was doing standing in between a wired-to-talk department store mannequin and this weird old man, in a room where just two days ago I thought there had been a murder.

But there was something sad and still sort of gingersnappy about Mr. Skeehan that I liked. "H — How did the President come to know about you having a letter from Abraham Lincoln, sir?" I asked.

"Told him," Mr. Skeehan said.

"But I mean how?" I said, determined to see this through.

"Wrote him a letter, missy," he said. "I wanted Mr. Abraham Lincoln's letter to get to a place it rightfully belonged in the history of our great South. Who could I trust to take care of that, if

I could not trust my own President?"

I started toward the door. "I have to go now," I said. "Tilford's waiting for me to go bike riding, but we *will* help you find your letter, honest."

Mr. Skeehan got up slowly, gave a big sigh, and came over to unlock the door for me.

As he turned the lock I touched his hand. "I already have a great idea about finding it," I promised. Before I even finished saying that, my forehead began to tickle. I don't know what made me tell that whopper. I guess I just felt powerful sorry for him, that's all.

I went on across the hall to check on Soon Gone. Just as I opened our door she leaped in through the open window next to the fire escape. Her ears were lying back like she was frightened. Then I saw there was something hanging from her neck. I dashed over to the windowsill and grabbed her up in my arms. There was a note tied around her neck with a piece of yarn!

I slipped the yarn off over her head and read the printed words: "Curiosity will kill the cat!"

I felt as if a cold wind had suddenly blown in and chilled me from head to toes. I looked out the window and down the fire escape, but there was no one in sight.

I closed the window and looked around the room. What should I do? Who could have written such a mean note? I took Soon Gone into my room and set her in the middle of my bed. I closed the door and went to the kitchen.

I stuck two apples in a sack along with some store-bought cookies and shut the apartment door real quietly behind me, so as not to let Soon Gone know I was leaving.

When I got to the second floor landing there was Mrs. Potts just disappearing through her door. Her empty trash basket sat where we had left it. Had Mrs. Potts written that note and tied it around Soon Gone's neck? Well, I certainly wasn't scared of *her*! I decided to wait until we got to the beach to mention the note to Tilford. Soon as I told him I suspected Mrs. Potts, he was sure to make some excuse for her.

I got my bike from behind the carport. As I rounded the corner of the house I called to Tilford, who was waiting out front, "Race you to the end of the lane and no fair taking a start ahead of me." He didn't answer.

In spite of the chill the note had given me, it was a warmly soft day. I had a sudden yearning to be on the beach. Soon Gone was safely closed up in my bedroom, and we wouldn't need to come back until toward evening when Mama would get home. She'd worry sure if I wasn't there.

I beat Tilford easily, but I was almost certain he had let me win. I was surprised, but then Tilford wasn't at all like any of the boys I was used to. In our old neighborhood there were lots of kids. Mostly the boys stayed off to themselves, but if a girl had challenged them to a race they'd do their lickin' best to beat her.

As we rode along Croker Sack Road I wondered if maybe having a father who was a clown made Tilford different. It was peaceful riding along, and the air was heavy with a nice salt and dead fish stink. Still it made me feel sort of uneasy to have Tilford not saying anything.

He still hadn't said a single word by the time we were passing Creepin' Charlie. I noticed that the swamp water was up. Whenever Mama and I had driven past the swamp there never was any water standing so you could see it. Now it was nearly covering the swamp grasses. Even the tall pickerelweed's blue flowers and heart-shaped leaves barely showed above the water. The pelicans were standing belly deep. I asked Tilford about it, but he just shrugged.

I told myself he was just enjoying the salty breeze blowing off the ocean same as I was. Still it made me uneasy because it wasn't like him.

In a few minutes he pulled his bike off the road a ways so I did, too. Then we walked down to the white roughness of the ocean's edge. By this time I was sure there was something wrong. I thought about telling Tilford how being this close to the ocean always made me feel like everything was going to turn out okay. Because it is so big, I guess, and because it's always *there*. Even though Tilford wasn't like other boys, I couldn't be sure he wouldn't think that was soupy. But it seemed like somebody ought to talk, so I said it.

Tilford picked up a clam shell and threw it far out across the choppy white-capped water. "Well, everything isn't going to turn out all right for my father," he said angrily. He reached down for another shell.

"What's wrong?" I asked.

"We just now got a letter telling him that in order to get into Clown College he has to make a trip to New York for tryouts."

"Is he scared he won't be one of the ones chosen?" I asked, pulling off my tennis shoes to wiggle my toes in the wet sand.

"Course not!" Tilford said almost like I'd said his father was a thief or something awful. "It's just that going to New York for the auditions will cost a lot of money, and we've been saving hard as we can for Clown College."

"Does your mom have a job?" I asked. "If she doesn't, likely she'd go to work to help out. You could stay alone same as me."

Tilford ducked his head and said, "My mother is dead. That's all there is to it, she's dead."

I got scared. I thought he was going to cry or something. He seemed to be trying to make a hundred different looking faces all at one time. "That's awful," I said, leaning down to get a throwing shell myself. I heaved it far out as I could. At least, I thought, my father isn't dead!

Tilford squared his shoulders. "Maybe my dad and your mama will meet sometime and decide to be friends," he said. "My dad's powerful lonesome, I can tell."

"No!" I said louder than I meant to. "No, I'm sure Mama wouldn't like that."

"You mean she wouldn't like my dad. You mean because he's a clown or something?" Tilford looked hopping mad.

"Course not!" I said quick as I could. "I didn't

go to make you mad. You don't understand."

"Then explain so as I do," Tilford demanded.

"Well, gee, I don't know — " I began. "It's just that my Mama, she — she just wouldn't." I didn't know how to get free of this tangle of words. I only knew I couldn't stand to think of Mama with anybody else but my father — not even if Tilford's father, when I finally met him, was as nice as Tilford himself. Just thinking about it made my stomach feel like a whirly-on-a-stick with a strong wind blowing.

"I'm going home," Tilford said, starting to walk off.

"Wait," I begged him. "See, it's just that my mama and dad well they — they well — My dad's comin' back — he's he's — but it's a secret. See, he misses us and — well, I know he's coming back!" The inside of my forehead tickled so bad from that lie that it was making my chin crinkle up.

"Hey! That's great!" Tilford said. "Why didn't you tell me sooner? I'm honest true glad for you, Dorinda. Come on, let's get going."

It didn't seem like the right time at all to tell him about the note around Soon Gone's neck. Nor the right time to remind him I had brought our lunch. As we picked up our bikes I said, "I'm sorry about your father worrying. I reckon most everybody worries about money."

We didn't talk on the ride home, either. Only then I had a reason to keep quiet. I was too miserable to talk. I'd said too much already. Tilford would expect my father to show up any day. The trouble with lies was they got said so easy, but there was no way to get them unsaid.

I told myself the lie was necessary. I couldn't have Tilford not liking me. He was the only friend I had around here. Anyway, maybe it was the truth. Maybe Dad would come back some day. But I knew in my heart he wouldn't, and I decided I truly did hate him for that.

10

Tilford didn't mention the tryouts for Clown College again. I didn't mention the note I'd found around Soon Gone's neck, either. I was sure it was Mrs. Potts who put it there, and I knew Tilford would make an excuse for her. But I decided to keep a close eye on Soon Gone.

I didn't see Tilford for the next three days because he went with his dad who was in a Semi-circus out on the Isle of the Palms. Tilford had told me that his dad was going to do an act where he squeezed into a Volkswagon with eighteen other clowns.

"They'll be stacked in criss-cross layers," he had explained proudly. "They even have a blueprint of each clown's size and weight. My dad is in the second row from the top."

"In one little Volkswagon?" I said. "Wow." I

didn't laugh, even though it made a funny picture in my mind because I knew by now that clowning was serious business.

"My dad says anyone can learn to do clown *tricks*," Tilford had explained. "He says what you can't learn is the heartfelt desire to be a circus clown — to want to make people laugh. My dad says clowns have to have hearts big as Alaska."

Since we moved out here, often as I had seen Tilford, I still hadn't met his father. In my mind I tried to picture what Tilford's dad looked like. But all I could see was a taller Tilford Jones with a painted clown face.

With Tilford gone, the big old rundown plantation called Winfield Place seemed lonely. Late afternoon of the third day he was gone, I went down and knocked on Miss Lizzie's door partly to have someone to talk to besides Soon Gone. But partly I wanted to see if she might say something that would be a clue to Mr. Skeehan's missing letter. I'd even planned some things I might say to lead her on toward mentioning him. But, of course, I couldn't mention the letter itself, having promised we wouldn't.

Miss Lizzie acted mighty pleased to see me. She told me to sit in her big blue-flowered chair. Her yellow cat was already asleep in it, but she shoo'd him right on out.

"His name is Havanonion," she told me. "My boy William gave him that name." Soon as I sat down, her cat hopped right back up onto my lap.

Miss Lizzie served me iced tea with fresh mint out of the yard. For a while we sat there talking about cats. At first I had trouble saying her cat's name, but she said, "Lordy, child, just say it like the words *have an onion*." That made it easy.

I didn't want to start right off asking questions about Mr. Skeehan for fear Miss Lizzie would think that was the main reason I came to visit her. So I told her about the high water I'd seen yesterday in Creepin' Charlie Swamp.

"Why, that's 'cause the moon and the sun, child, they both on the same side of the Earth," she said. "That makes the water in old Creepin' Charlie rise, but don't ask me why."

"Oh," I said. Then for a minute neither of us said anything. I just smoothed the fur on Havanonion's long flat side. Truth was I was trying to think of just the right way to lead around to Mr. Skeehan. At last I said, "Mr. Skeehan across the hall, he sure seems lonely. I reckon he doesn't have any family or friends at all — to come see him."

"Now, I don't know about that, honey," Miss Lizzie said. "Don't go frettin' yourself too bad for him. Hardly more than a week ago, you know, somebody sent him flowers. He must have someone who cares."

So, I thought, that florist card I picked up must have fallen out of Mr. Skeehan's trash! I felt good, knowing he wasn't really alone in the world.

Seemed like there wasn't anything more to say about him to keep that conversation going. But it was easy to talk to Miss Lizzie. Somehow she approved of 'most anything I said. I asked her if it was okay if I picked some pecans for Mama from the trees down 'round the old slave quarters.

"Pshaw, child, yes," she said. "And long's you're about it, pick me up a few."

I promised I would. I couldn't think what to say next so I got up to go, but almost like she wanted to keep me there for company, Miss Lizzie began telling me about when her grandaddy was a boy and lived in the quarters by those pecan trees. I sat back down.

"My grandaddy was the white man's favorite,"

she said with a chuckle. "He taught my grandaddy how to read and write. That white man being old Mr. Winfield, you see. Mrs. Winfield herself couldn't do either one. She was too busy being a fine lady to study on book learning."

Miss Lizzie sure seemed to be enjoying the telling of this story. She went on, "Now old Mr. Winfield, they tell, was kind of crippled up, but proudlike, you see. He wouldn't hear about using a cane. When my grandaddy was just a tadpole he was the right height for that old man to lay his hand there on the top of that child's head and steady himself wherever he went."

Miss Lizzie chuckled, and I laughed, too, at the picture this made inside my mind. It was getting almost time for Mama, so I said I better be going.

I thanked Miss Lizzie for a right nice time and promised I'd be back another day.

"There's a letter for your mama in the basket in the hall," Miss Lizzie said as I started out the door. She checked outside her door like she had that first time we came here. Knowing how snoopy that Mrs. Potts was, I was beginning to understand why Miss Lizzie did this.

I went out through the stained glass door to the halltree where the letter basket hung. Sure enough there was a letter addressed to Mama from my brother Lance.

I tucked the envelope inside my T-shirt and started for our apartment. I hadn't really gotten any clues from Miss Lizzie about Mr. Skeehan's missing letter, but at least I didn't have to feel so sorry for him anymore.

He had a relative or friend who cared enough about him to send flowers. Maybe that person would help pay for his eye operation. That is if Mr. Skeehan wasn't too peppery proud to accept help.

I gave Mama her letter as soon as she got inside our door good, figuring it would make her happy. But when she finished reading it she dropped her hand to her side like the letter was too heavy to hold onto and said, "Lance and Jim Joe have been to spend a couple of days with your father. Your father has explained to them that he has filed for a divorce because I refused to."

"But he — " I began. I started over, "But Mama, we — " I couldn't say what I was thinking: *He can't! We need him.* I just looked at Mama and felt like I had swallowed a bay oyster whole.

After that, Mama and I were both carrying the blues around inside us for sure. To cheer Mama I said, "After we eat, why don't we go down and visit with Miss Lizzie a while. She's nice, Mama." Mama shook her head. I knew if she felt as bad inside as I did, nothing was going to help. Still I couldn't give up trying. Mama needed me now worse than ever.

"Or better yet," I said, "let's you and me go over to South Beach and have us a nice supper. Being at the ocean might help."

"Honey," Mama said, looking around the living room like it was a cell with bars keeping her in, "I know I'm failing you. Almost as bad as — *he* did." She went over to the fire escape window. "This dark old house; you bein' all alone all day long and not really knowin' anyone here."

I went over beside her and squeezed her around the waist. "You got no right saying that, Mama," I said fiercely. "You and me — we'll always stick together. And you're wrong about the house! I do have friends here. I have Mr. Skeehan right across the hall. He likes me. And Tilford Jones I told you about. And there's a school teacher — or she used to be." It's true, I assured myself, Miss Kate is almost my friend. My forehead only tickled a little bit. "And Miss Lizzie truly admires me to visit with her. See, Mama," I finished up,

"I have all kinds of friends here already." Of course I didn't add Mrs. Potts, the snoop, to my list.

Mama brushed my bangs off my forehead and acted like she was really seeing me. "I haven't made this easy, have I, Sisterbaby?" she said softly.

Before I thought, I pulled away and said, "Don't call me that!" Right away I knew that had hurt her so I tacked on quick, "I'm getting too old for that name anyhow."

Mama took a deep breath. "You feed Soon Gone," she said. "I'll be ready soon's you've finished, and we'll do that — go to South Beach, I mean. Okay?"

"Okay," I said, feeling some better for thinking about being near the powerful ocean.

11

That night, home in bed, I dreamed about my dad for the second time since he left us. It was a good dream with him living with us just as if nothing had happened. Only thing was we lived in a strange house with lots of rooms and I kept trying to find Dad in one room after another.

Next morning I was awake even before the birds began singing their first-light song. I couldn't stop thinking about my dad really never coming back to Mama and me. Finally I got up and went out and started breakfast for the two of us.

Mama looked poorly so I knew she hadn't slept much, either. After she had gone to work I went downstairs and hung around out front hoping I'd see Tilford. Miss Lizzie came out with her yard broom, and I offered to do the sweeping for her.

"Now, child, that's mighty nice of you," she said, handing me her gallberry brush broom. "I reckon I'll just sit down here and rest these old knees a bit."

While I was still sweeping at the sandy yard, Mr. Skeehan came walking up the tabby drive. Miss Lizzie had told me he had a ride out Croker Sack Road far as our lane.

"Morning, sir," I said, smiling at him. I stopped sweeping so as not to stir up dust while he went by. He looked dreadful tired, but he smiled back at me like we shared a secret, which of course we did.

He went inside the entry hall and I could see him through the open door as he lifted the seat to the halltree where the mail basket hung. He reached in and took out his neatly folded Confederate flag. He came back to the porch and set the flag carefully in the brown jug like always. He nodded at Miss Lizzie and then looked at me. "Saying you all have time," he said, "will you and Tilford Jones come up to my place for a minute this morning?"

"Sure," I said, feeling important. "We'll be up soon as I see him." Seemed like the folks around here truly were getting to like me. I'd been right when I told Mama I had good and plenty of friends already.

After Mr. Skeehan went inside, Miss Lizzie said, "Far as that goes, I myself would favor a mess of marsh marigold greens boiled up with a piece of salt pork. Next time you and Tilford ride up Croker Sack Road stop at the edge of Creepin' Charlie and fetch me a bunch, will you?"

I was squatting to pull up a clump of sedge grass sprouting around the foot scraper, so luckily she didn't see me wrinkle my nose at the thought of eating marsh marigolds. "Sure we will," I said.

"You'll find them growing along the edge. They like to keep their feet wet without going overboard. Should be tender buds now. Fetch me stems and all."

"Yes, ma'am, we rightly will," I promised. I liked being around Miss Lizzie. She made me feel better about what Lance had said in his letter. She made me feel like I still sort of had a family after all.

Just as I finished sweeping, Tilford came out the front door. Right behind him was a man I supposed was his father. Turned out it was. I was glad to be finding out what he was like at last.

Tilford's father was shorter and thinner than I

had pictured him. He didn't look a thing like Tilford. He was a little bit stoop shouldered and had a friendly mouth. He had thinking eyes. He didn't look at all like a clown, either.

Tilford had a big smile on his face and I thought, he's as proud of his father as I used to be of mine. I felt the ugly weight of jealousy in my bones. All the good feeling I'd had being with Miss Lizzie was gone.

Tilford took his father's hand and led him over to where I was standing still holding the yard broom. He looked proud as if he had *invented* fathers! "Dorinda," he began formal-like in that way that made me wonder if he was trying to be funny or serious, "I'm pleased to introduce my father to you. His name is Gifford Jones, but he's better known as Happy the Clown." (As if I didn't know that!) "Dad, this is my friend Dorinda Saunders."

Be nice, I warned myself, or you'll be sorry. It's not Tilford's fault your dad left you. But I could feel that my smile didn't reach my eyes.

Mr. Jones shook my hand acting as serious as Tilford. "Pleased to meet you, Miss Dorinda," he said. Then he said good morning to Miss Lizzie. I pictured him in my mind dressed like a clown with makeup on his face. It was hard because he just looked like an ordinary man dressed to go to work. He and Tilford went down the steps and around toward the carport.

I thought about Mr. Skeehan wanting us to come talk to him. I wondered if he'd want just me. It would serve Tilford right, I thought watching the two of them disappear around the corner of the house, if I found the Lincoln letter by myself.

It turned out Tilford's father drove off by himself down the tabby lane in his rusty old jeep. When the jeep was out of sight Tilford came back to the porch. I felt right guilty about what I'd been thinking. I told him that Mr. Skeehan wanted to see us. "I wonder if maybe he has a clue about his — "

I stopped as Tilford rolled his eyes toward Miss Lizzie in a silent signal not to go talking about Mr. Skeehan's letter where she could hear.

I looked quickly at Miss Lizzie, but she hadn't seemed to notice. She just said, "Thank you, child," as I handed her the broom. I supposed she was thanking me for sweeping, but I pretended she was really thanking me for being her friend.

Tilford and I went on inside and up to the third

floor. I knocked on Mr. Skeehan's door, careful to miss the Southern Patriot Lives Here sign. We heard him stumble over something as he came to answer my knock.

"I'm obliged you came," he said, holding the door open just enough for us to come through. The mannequin was still standing there in his spanking new shoes and too-short pants. It was easier to believe he was there to keep Mr. Peter Skeeter company than that he was there to protect him from being robbed again.

"There's something come to my mind about my letter," Mr. Skeehan began as soon as the locks were back in place. "Sit here." He motioned to his table, and we all three sat in the straight chairs. The worn leather cash book his mother had kept her journal in was still lying on the table.

"What is it, sir?" Tilford asked.

"A real clue," Mr. Skeehan said proudly. "That pot of flowers over there." He pointed to a pot of droopy chrysanthemums in one corner of the room. "I plumb forgot about it until today. It showed up here the same day the letter was stolen. I noticed right away that my letter was gone because the thief had left Mother's journal open. I started looking around. The only other thing different was that pot of flowers. The thief must have left them."

"Are you sure you locked your door when you went to work that night?" Tilford asked.

"See here, young fella," Mr. Peter Skeeter said, "I am a night watchman. I know a locked door when I see one."

"I didn't go to be insulting you," Tilford said with such a sorry look on his face that I changed the subject fast as I could.

"Maybe the thief came through the window," I said.

Mr. Skeehan shook his head. "I checked on that, too, missy. The nail was still in place the same as it was until the day you two broke in — "

I held my breath. For a second I thought he was going to scold us again for breaking in that day. But he pulled off his glasses, wiped his eyes and added, "and saved my life."

I could tell it was hard for him to admit he'd been so helpless when after all, being a deputized night watchman was almost the same as being a policeman. I changed the subject again. "It's too bad the card that came with the flowers didn't have the florist's name on it."

Mr. Skeehan looked at me puzzled like, so I

explained. "The little florist card — it fell out of the trash last Friday. But I picked it up!" I added quickly remembering how secretive some of the folks here were about their trash.

"There wasn't any card in those flowers. I *looked*," Mr. Skeehan said in a positive voice. "Don't know who sent me the fool plant."

I looked at Tilford. I imagined he felt the same as I did, that with Mr. Skeehan's eyes being so bad, he must not have noticed the card. But I sure wasn't going to risk questioning his word again.

"It's plain," I said, skipping over the awkward moment, "that whoever delivered the flowers stole your Lincoln letter. All we have to do is find out what florist shop those flowers came from."

"But how could the delivery man get inside," Tilford said, "and then lock the door behind himself?"

"Miss Lizzie could have given him the key because she can't climb the stairs anymore," I said, remembering what she'd said that first day we had looked at our apartment.

But Mr. Skeehan was shaking his head. "When not even one soul in this house knew about the letter, how could a delivery man with a pot of flowers know exactly where to find it — even know I had it? Like I said, not one other thing in my place had been disturbed. It's like the ghost of Abraham Lincoln came back and took his letter away himself."

Mr. Skeehan looked so discouraged I felt like putting my arm around his shoulder. If he really had been my grandfather I couldn't have wanted more to find his letter and make things right for him again.

I had only known Mr. Skeehan a little while, but already I cared a lot about him getting his chance to have his eyes fixed so he could see better and keep his job.

He rubbed his forehead. "Time I got some sleep, young'uns," he said. He got up slowly and went over and unlocked the door for us.

"Don't you worry, sir," Tilford said in a whisper as we went out his door, "Dorinda and I will — "

Tilford stopped right there. I looked in the direction he was looking just in time to see the back of Mrs. Potts's head disappearing down the third floor stairway.

12

I yelled good-bye at Tilford and Mr. Skeehan and dashed into our apartment to make sure Soon Gone was safe. She was curled up asleep on the davenport and the fire escape window was closed. I grabbed her up and held her so tight she meowed and jumped down and began smoothing her fur with her tongue.

That afternoon Tilford and I rode our bikes up Croker Sack Road to Creepin' Charlie Swamp to fetch Miss Lizzie's marsh marigold greens. Taking them to her would give us an excuse to ask her about the delivery man who had brought Mr. Skeehan's plant. Also to find out if she had given him the key and let him go up alone.

Since the marsh marigolds weren't quite blossomed out yet I couldn't tell them from all the millions of other wild stuff growing there. The only plant I could call by name was the pitcher plant with its flat snakelike head rising even higher than the swamp grasses.

But Tilford claimed he could tell the marigolds by the leaves. And sure enough the first one he picked had a tiny tight greenish white bud. We picked a mess of them and I carried them in my bike basket.

As we were going in the door at Winfield House, Tilford said, "We'll ask Miss Lizzie about the delivery man real casual-like so as not to have her ask why we want to know."

Miss Lizzie opened the door wide soon as she saw it was us. She seemed right pleased to get the greens. "Just let me put them in water," she said. "You can come in and set a spell."

I picked up Havanonion from his favorite chair and held him on my lap while we visited. Tilford was sitting cross-legged on the carpet. Though his face was serious, sitting like that, I could almost picture him in my mind in clown clothes. All at once, out of the corner of my eye I saw a shadow pass outside Miss Lizzie's window. Was that Mrs. Potts snooping around again? Just then Miss Lizzie came back from putting the greens to soak, and I forgot about the shadow.

So as to bring up Mr. Peter Skeeter's name, I said, "I wonder if Mr. Skeehan would like some marsh marigold greens next time we pass by there."

"Most likely he would," Miss Lizzie said shaking her head. "Sakes, but he's been looking poorly lately."

"Yes, ma'am," Tilford agreed. "You know he worries a lot. Take for instance, he worries how that pot of flowers got inside his place when his door was locked."

"No need of that worry," Miss Lizzie said. "They came at night while he was working. I gave the delivery man the extra key since my old knees — "

I got so excited I broke in, "What did he look like — the delivery man, I mean?" I heard my voice trail off as I looked at Tilford, realizing I'd said too much too fast.

"Lordy, child," Miss Lizzie said, "I do remember thinking that fellow was a sorry sight. Skinny — pale with pale hair. He was wearing one long dangly earring. I declare I just don't . . ."

I stopped hearing her words. The earring! Of course. The man I'd seen that day parked in the lane spying on Winfield House! I shivered inside remembering his skinny face, his little eyes watching me. Somehow I knew he was the thief. I couldn't wait to talk to Tilford alone.

"We'd better go," I said, looking hard at Tilford. I stood up lifting Havanonion and putting him back in his chair. "I promised Mama I'd start some red rice to soaking," I explained to Miss Lizzie. I felt the old familiar tickle in my forehead, but I just had to get out of there and talk to Tilford before I burst.

Soon as Miss Lizzie closed her door behind us, I said, remembering the shadow outside Miss Lizzie's window, "We'd better go up to my place to talk." I also had in mind to go ahead and soak some red rice and tell Mama I was just hungry for it. But then I realized that wouldn't be exactly truthful, either — which I was trying powerful hard to be because I had promised God one night, that if he'd stop my father from truly getting a divorce, I would stop telling lies. Even little ones.

The minute we had closed our door I said, "Tilford, I know that delivery man!"

"Who is he?" Tilford looked excited.

"I don't know, but I saw him — almost the very first day I came here, parked halfway down our

lane watching this house. He was mean looking —
I know he's the thief!"

Tilford caught his upper lip with his teeth and
scowled. "How could some delivery man know
where the letter was kept? Even know about the
letter in the first place?"

"He might have found it accidentally," I said.
"Maybe he was just looking around, saw that journal book lying there, and opened it. Then he saw
the letter. Yes!" I decided out loud, "That's it!"

"Could be," Tilford admitted. "But we don't
have any proof. We don't even know who the man
is or where to find him."

"He's been here twice before," I said. "He may
show up again any day now. And if he does — "

"What?" Tilford said. "What can we do?"

I didn't have any answer right then. Tilford left
after saying he thought we ought not to think
about all this until tomorrow. But I could tell from
the way he was acting that he didn't plan to actually *do* anything.

I went to the kitchen and got down the canister
where Mama kept the rice. I thought, if only
Lance or Jim Joe were here — or Dad. I felt angry
and hopeless inside. And of course, I didn't dare

ask Mama for help. She'd worry up a storm about the whole thing.

There's only me to help Mr. Skeehan, I thought. I just have to do something. If I see that man again, I *will* do something, I promised myself.

13

The next day Tilford left to go to what he called the Cream City Semi-circus where his father had a clown job. Tilford was excited because his father was going to let him help with one of his acts.

I kept an eye out for the shiny car to be parked down our lane, but I didn't see it again, either.

One morning a couple of days before Tilford was supposed to get back to Winfield House, a damp clam of fog settled down over the plantation. It made me feel smothery and sad. I decided to go down and visit with Miss Lizzie. I thought maybe she was feeling closed in because of the fog same as I was.

Even after I knocked I didn't have a living notion in my mind what I was going to visit about.

I wouldn't have needed to worry about that

because when Miss Lizzie saw it was me she said, "Come inside, child, this minute, you hear! I do believe the good Lord has sent you down to this black lady this blessed morning."

I was mighty pleased to be so strongly welcomed. I'd gotten so I liked the feeling inside Miss Lizzie's place with the lazy old Havanonion drowsing in the flowered chair. The air today smelled of bread baking.

"I just came down to sort of visit," I said. Somehow with Miss Lizzie it was hard to say the wrong things, because she seemed so steady and so approving.

"I declare, I don't know what I would have done if you hadn't happened to come by, young'un," she said. Then she took a man-sized hanky out of her apron pocket and gave her nose a good blow. She stuffed the hanky back into her pocket and looked at me with her whole hand covering her lips as if she was studying me. At last she said, "I have a letter that — "

She hesitated, looking almost guilty. Had Miss Lizzie stolen Mr. Skeehan's letter! No, that was impossible.

"Truth is, child," Miss Lizzie went on as she

wrapped her arms in her apron, "I can't read. This letter — it's from my boy William."

I was surprised how glad I felt to know for positive Miss Lizzie wasn't the thief. I guess I looked surprised because she seemed to think she needed to explain the letter to me.

"My William went to college," she said looking proud. "He's the one bought this place. He's a fine boy and works for our government. He's what they call a cartographer. That means he makes maps. He makes maps about defense of our country. 'Course he knows I can't read what he writes me. But he doesn't know Mayella's gone into the city to live now. She used to read his letters for me."

"I'll read it you," I jumped in. I wasn't the world's champion reader, but if the words were too long or hard I could sound them out.

Miss Lizzie unrolled her arms from her apron and fetched out a letter from the pocket. It had been folded and refolded around its envelope. On the inside of the folds was a check. I was relieved to see the letter was typed. I'm not too good at reading some people's cursive.

The letter wasn't very long.

Dear Mama, (I read out loud)

I hope you are feeling stronger by now. Did the medicine help your knees?

Get ready for a big surprise. The first of the children is on her way to you. Her name is Poppy. You need to be prepared. She has been badly abused, and you will see some scars. She has never been outside of New York City — probably never been far off the block where she was born.

She's shy and scared like they all are, and, Mama, there are so many of them needing our help.

But this is the first little black angel and more will be sent for their stay with you in that wonderful sea air.

This is what you and I dreamed and planned for, Mama. I'm counting on you to know what to do, because you have always known how to heal with your love.

I love you, Mama.

William

Then there was a P.S. which I read,

The enclosed check for one hundred dollars is for the extra food you'll need — we're sending her with plenty of clothes. A Mrs. Stucky in Charleston will meet her train and put her in a Yellow Cab right up to your front door. I'll send more money soon.

When I looked up from reading, Miss Lizzie was laughing and crying all at the same time. "Praise the Lord!" she cried, hugging me. "He's sending them to me at last." Then she let go and reached for her handkerchief again.

My head was crammed with questions, but I couldn't think where to start.

"My boy William," Miss Lizzie went on, "does volunteer work to help poor children. You have heard about that, I just know. It's our plan someday, when he has enough money, to quit working — to fill this big old plantation house with these children who never really had homes of their own. I've asked the Lord to let me live to see that day!"

"But now one is really coming here?" I asked, handing her the letter and walking slowly over to pet Havanonion.

"Lordy yes, child," Miss Lizzie said. "One is sure enough coming right here to this old house. And she will live for a whole month, or maybe longer if they don't place her in a good home by then, right here with Havanonion and me. I've got beds all set up and waiting for the poor little souls. Little black angels, my boy William calls them. And you got to be nice to her, you hear? Everybody does or they'll have me to account to." She laughed and hugged me again.

Her happiness seemed to be filling the rooms and overflowing. The sun even came out and was streaming in through the two narrow front windows by her table. But her happiness didn't seem to include me.

Would Miss Lizzie still want me to come down to visit her when her black angel got here? I was certain sure she wouldn't when she said, "You scoot along now, child. I got plenty to do without you hindering me." Even though she hugged me again, it felt almost like a good-bye hug.

14

The very next day she came — the girl in the letter. I was sitting alone on the porch step when the yellow taxi came up our tabby lane and stopped almost in front of me.

A girl about my age only taller got out of the back seat. She was thin and mighty pretty. I knew right off this was Miss Lizzie's first black angel. But I sure couldn't see any scars.

Before the cab driver had finished setting down her new-looking suitcase and a box, Miss Lizzie came bustling out the front door.

"Mercy, mercy, mercy," she was crying as she hurried past me and down the two steps toward the new girl. When she reached her, she hugged the girl, suitcase and all.

"Lordy sakes, child, you must be plumb worn out," she was saying as she half led, half pulled the new girl right on past me as if I wasn't even there.

But then I guess Miss Lizzie remembered what she had said about me being nice to her, because she stopped at the front door and said, "Dorinda, you all come on up here."

When I started toward them, the girl moved closer to Miss Lizzie almost like she was scared of me. And yet when I got real close I saw an I-dare-you-to-get-in-my-way look in her eyes.

I said, "Hey," right nicely and then I couldn't think of a cotton-pickin' thing more to say.

Miss Lizzie said, "This young lady is Poppy who William spoke of in his letter. Poppy, this is Dorinda. Her and her mama live up on the third floor. Now I know you two will get on fine as goose down." Then Miss Lizzie turned, opened the door and the two of them, along with the box and suitcase, went inside.

I felt shut out. Probably now Miss Lizzie won't even need my help reading letters, I decided, now that she's got Poppy. Well, who needs her? I said to myself. I've got Mama and Mama has me, and we don't need another person in this whole world.

Of course, there was Tilford Jones. Tilford was certainly my friend. I wondered would Tilford like

Poppy better than he liked me. She was certainly prettier. I knew he would likely be friends with her. Tilford seemed to like everyone. Even that snoopy Mrs. Potts.

I woke up early the next morning and looked out the fire escape window to see if Mr. Jones's jeep was back in its usual parking place alongside the carport.

It was. So as soon as Mama left for work I went down to the front steps hoping Tilford would come out. I'd really be glad to see him. I wanted to talk to him about the new girl.

Instead it was the new girl herself who came out the front door. I remembered what Miss Lizzie had warned me about being nice, so I tried right off. "How do you like it here at Winfield Plantation?" I asked her.

"Stinks," she said leaning boredlike against one paint-peeled column.

I glanced back toward Miss Lizzie's window, hoping she hadn't heard. "Don't you like Miss Lizzie?" I whispered hardly able to believe her.

"She's okay if you like old ladies," Poppy said. "What's it to you?"

I thought about how excited Miss Lizzie had been about Poppy coming here in the first place.

What would happen to her dream of filling this whole big house with children? I had to keep trying to make her like us.

"Wait till you meet Tilford Jones," I said. "You'll for certain sure like him."

Poppy rolled her eyes upward and said in a bored voice, "I have. Just a little while ago."

"Don't you like him, either?" I asked.

"He's a liar," she said, "and I told him so. I happen to *live* in New York City, and there's no such thing as tryouts for Clown College. Far as that goes there's no such thing as Clown College. I ought to know. What's that thing?" she asked, pointing at the brown jug with Mr. Skeehan's flag propped in it.

"It's the Confederate flag," I said, feeling like there'd be no use explaining about Mr. Skeehan. He was my friend, and I didn't want her making fun of him, too.

"Weird," she said. "Don't you Southerners know the Civil War is over?" Then she pointed down to the slave quarters. "What are those stupid-looking buildings that look like they're stuck together with shells?"

"They're oyster shells," I said, "and those are historic buildings. They're the old slave quarters."

"You jivin' me!" she said.

"No, honest. Miss Lizzie's very own grandfather grew up in one of those buildings. She told me so."

Poppy gave me a little shove. "Up North blacks were free. New Yorkers never kept people slaves," she said. "Only you poor white trash Southerners did mean things like that."

I looked back at the door wishing mightily that Tilford would come out. I didn't know whether there used to be slaves in New York or not. But I had made up my mind to be nice to this girl for Miss Lizzie's sake, and there was nothing to do but to ignore this insult.

"Want to ride bikes?" I asked. I looked at her denim skirt and white shirt. "You could change. I'd wait. Maybe we could borrow Tilford's and ride up to Creepin' Charlie Swamp together."

"Riding bikes is for children," she said. "In New York I drive a car. Alone. And I certainly don't want to spend my time hanging out at some dirty old swamp — Creepin' Charlie. Ha! I'll bet." She turned and dashed inside the front door. But as she turned I thought I saw tears flooding her eyes.

15

Seemed like Poppy no more got inside the door good before Miss Lizzie came marching out it.

"Now you listen here, child," she said sitting down on the top step beside me. "I told you before, you going to be friends with Poppy. Don't you go makin' her cry no more, hear?"

"But," I spluttered so surprised I couldn't talk. I almost said, She doesn't even like you, but I didn't because I wanted mightily for Miss Lizzie not to be hurt.

"Now tell me honest, did you make fun of her like she said?" Miss Lizzie scolded.

"I swear I didn't," I said, raising my hand palm out.

"What made her cry then?" Miss Lizzie demanded.

"I declare, I don't know!" I said.

Miss Lizzie wouldn't give up. "Now you and me going to get to the undersides of this here and now. What did you say?"

"Honest, Miss Lizzie," I said, "all I did was ask her to go bike riding up to Creepin' Charlie."

Miss Lizzie covered her lips with her plump brown hand and looked like she was thinking. Then she nodded. "That child likely never had a bike. Likely never rode one. She just too proud to say so. Not easy being dirt poor — no mama, no daddy."

"But she could have just said so," I said. I didn't like Miss Lizzie blaming me for something I didn't go to do.

"And she sobbin' about alligators. Now ain't alligators in Creepin' Charlie!"

"But I didn't say — "

"You mean to tell me, child, you never said the word alligator?" Miss Lizzie demanded.

"I swear," I said.

"Land sakes, that poor child must be scared of everything around here. Used to the city like she is. You mind you'd be scared in a big city like New York, and I would. What with muggin' and all like I hear about on TV."

I didn't say anything. But I wanted to say how

Poppy had lied that she drove a car alone in New York. I bit my lip not to.

Miss Lizzie touched my arm. "I'm sorry I came at you so. I was counting big on you and Tilford to see that Poppy had a good time here."

I thought about how excited Miss Lizzie had been about these kids from the city coming here. I felt bad inside because even though I'd been nice enough to Poppy, I hadn't really liked her because she'd changed everything between Miss Lizzie and me just when we were getting to be good friends.

"I'll make her like me," I promised Miss Lizzie. "Some way I'll just make her like me."

But I didn't see Poppy again the rest of that day. It was Friday and soon as Tilford came out, we went up to pick up people's trash.

Tilford went on up to the third floor to get Mr. Skeehan's trash, and I went to pick up Miss Kate's and Mr. Digsby's. By then, when I heard a door creaking open behind me as I passed the second floor, I could tell if it was Miss Kate's door, Mr. Digby's, or Mrs. Potts's below us. If it was Mrs. Potts's I kept going. But no matter which of the other two it was, I would turn and wave to them figuring they didn't see that many people and were glad to hear someone going past even if it was only me.

Miss Kate would always give me a tiny brittle nod, but it was sort of approving — like I'd made a good grade in her classroom that day. One time she beckoned me over to her door and gave me a folder full of construction paper. I was planning to make her a present from it someday.

When I waved at Mr. Digsby, he would smile his shy shadow smile so I knew he liked and trusted me. This morning he didn't even bother to warn me not to spill any of his trash on the way down. Tilford would pick up Mrs. Potts's trash, which as usual, was sitting outside her door, and also Miss Lizzie's.

When we finished with the trash, Tilford and I set up a kind of office in one of the slave quarter buildings. I brought the construction paper Miss Kate had given me and all the pencils and pens I could find. Tilford brought paste and some important looking paper that he said used to be in his grandfather's office when his grandfather was alive.

I was hoping Poppy wouldn't show up, because I knew she'd feel it was childish to pretend we were office workers. I decided not to mention her to Tilford because he seemed sort of quiet again, not like himself. Finally he told me it was because his father was still worrying about having the money to go to New York for clown tryouts which were only three months away. I was glad I hadn't mentioned Poppy, who had claimed there wasn't such a thing in New York as clown tryouts.

Then I didn't see Tilford or Poppy over the weekend. Saturday Mama and I drove in to Charleston to buy our next week's groceries. After that Mama had errands to do.

Sunday Mama and I got up early and went to South Beach and had a long day together in the sunshine. Like Mama said, "To heal our bones of their sorrow." I didn't say so, but my sorrow was mostly a tattered sort of anger at my father.

But Mama and I had each other for a whole long day. We ate pizza and watermelon at the far end of the pier, while the sea gulls and pelicans dipped and floated around us. I made up my mind not to worry about anything all day. Not even making friends with Poppy for Miss Lizzie's sake.

But Monday, soon as Mama left for work, I went down to the second floor and knocked on Tilford's door. I figured if anybody could help me make

friends with Miss Lizzie's Poppy, it would be Tilford — even if Poppy didn't like him. After all, I
hadn't thought I liked Tilford that first day,
either.

Mr. Jones answered my knock. "Tilford is still
eating his breakfast," he said, smiling at me. I
started to turn away, but he said, "No, come on
in and wait for him. I was just wishing someone
would knock on my door. Step into my parlor and
be my audience."

Mr. Jones was holding a giant bubble pipe. On
a table by the window there was a big red and
blue striped bowl full of thick-looking liquid.

"Bubble sculpture," Mr. Jones said, smiling this
time so wide that suddenly right in front of my
eyes he seemed to turn into Happy the Clown.

I watched as he dipped the big bubble pipe into
the bowl and blew on it. Out came a square bubble!
He lowered it carefully onto a wet newspaper
lying on the table. Then he dipped the pipe again
and blew a smaller square bubble. I held my
breath as he stacked the second square bubble
onto the top of the first bubble. Without even
planning to, I started clapping and cheering.

Tilford came in from the kitchen chewing the

last bite of his breakfast. He started clapping, too, and just as he did, both bubbles burst with a fairy-like ping!

Mr. Jones bowed the way Tilford always did and backed himself right out of the room toward the kitchen.

"Want to ride up the road a ways? Maybe to the beach?" I asked Tilford. "We've got a problem." I wasn't sure if I should have used *we* or not.

"Guess you mean Poppy," Tilford said, looking cross. "I *do* agree there's a problem. But, Dorinda, it's Poppy who has the problem, not you or me."

I knew well and good how Tilford felt about his father. And I knew the worst thing Poppy could have done was to practically call Tilford's father a liar about Clown College. But since Poppy didn't even have a father — same as me — I sort of knew how she felt, too. Besides — there was my promise to Miss Lizzie.

"I know what you mean, Tilford," I said, "but I promised Miss Lizzie I'd help Poppy have a good time here. Truth is, or at least Miss Lizzie says, Poppy is afraid of things out here away from the city — about riding bikes and going to swamps, see?"

"No, I don't," Tilford said. "Anyway, today I'm going to help my dad, so you go make friends with her, Dorinda."

I was surprised at the way Tilford was acting. It's usually him instead of me who makes excuses for people's bad behavior. But there wasn't anything for me to do, except leave.

16

Just before Tilford closed his door, I called back, "Do you mind if we borrow your bike then?" I felt put out at Tilford. He wasn't acting like himself at all. I'd counted on him to help me make friends with Poppy. I even had what I hoped was a good idea. Now I'd have to try out my idea by myself.

" 'Course not," Tilford called back and shut his door. I felt like he was shutting me out of his world same as Miss Lizzie.

I took a deep breath and went down and knocked on Miss Lizzie's door fast before I lost my courage. Poppy opened it. She didn't look quite so uppity as before. That gave me the nerve to say what I'd been rehearsing all the way down from Tilford's door, "Poppy, if you will teach me how to drive a car when I come to New York, I'll teach you to ride a bike." I held my breath. I wasn't sure what she'd do.

She looked at me with her nose level with my eyes like she was measuring me and said, "You're going to have to grow some, girl, just to see over the steering wheel."

I wasn't going to give up so easy. "That's okay, we won't be in New York for a while yet anyway," I said. The tickling began. So as to be honest I added, "If ever."

To my ever-lasting relief Poppy broke out laughing, so I laughed, too. "It's a deal then," she said.

I saw Miss Lizzie peeking around the corner of her kitchen as we left, and it made me feel good.

We went out back and got just my bike at first. The goldenrain tree was still shedding and Poppy asked me what those little pinkish pods were. I was right proud to be able to explain, but I tried hard not to sound proud. I knew there'd be lots of things in New York City that would need explaining to me — in case I ever did get to go there.

Poppy took to bike riding right off. In a couple of hours she was able to balance on her own. I could tell by the smile in her eyes she was plumb pleased with herself.

Then we brought Tilford's bike out to the tabby lane. By the time Poppy and I had ridden together up to Creepin' Charlie and back, we were laughing and talking. It was hard to believe we'd been enemies a few days ago.

We put the bikes up and as we came through the front hall, Miss Lizzie opened her door and called to Poppy to come in to lunch. Poppy turned and said, "See you after lunch?"

I got a secret smile feeling inside me. "Sure," I said.

Soon as Poppy had gone through the doorway, Miss Lizzie made a little circle with her thumb and forefinger, raised it in a little salute and winked at me. It looked like Poppy and I might get to be friends after all. I felt mighty good. I couldn't wait to see Tilford to tell him how nice Poppy really was now that she knew us better.

As I started up the steps, I remembered I hadn't given Soon Gone any breakfast. She was sure to be unhappy with me. I expected her to meet me at the door with disapproving meows. But she was nowhere in sight.

I called to her, but she didn't come. Then I saw that the fire escape window was open!

I ran to the window and looked down. No cat!

My mouth was so dry, I couldn't swallow as I pushed the curtain aside and climbed through the window. All the time running through my head were the words, "Curiosity will kill the cat." I tried to tell myself maybe Soon Gone was only out trying to find a field mouse for her breakfast.

I no more than took one step down the fire escape before I heard voices — a man's and a woman's. The man's voice sounded angry. I tightened my hold on the railing as I realized the voices reminded me of the ones Mama and I heard the first day we came here. They were coming from Mrs. Potts's apartment directly below me.

Even though my knees felt like jointed puppets I kept going down. When I actually came to the halfway landing I saw Mrs. Potts's window was open. Mrs. Potts had her back to me. But even not seeing her face I could tell she was scared.

I couldn't see the man. I could only hear his angry voice. "You the same as stole my money — an old lady like you gambling it away! Now you either get me that letter or — " As he said this he stomped out of the shadows toward Mrs. Potts with his hand raised in a fist. It was the man in the shiny car! The man with the dangly earring! The florist's delivery man!

17

My hands felt clammy cold on the fire escape's iron railing. My only thought was to unlock my knees and get moving on past that window as fast as I could.

But I seemed to be like a person caught in a snapshot forced to stand there forever. I heard Mrs. Potts say, "I tell you those two kids know too much. I listened outside Miss Lizzie's window one day when they were visiting her, and they asked all kind of questions about a delivery man. They're on to us sure as anything."

Kids! She must mean Tilford and me! That made me go so weak I lost my grip on the fire escape and was able to duck down out of their sight at last.

Just then I heard Poppy call my name. Before I looked down I glanced through the window to see if Mrs. Potts or the man had heard Poppy. They were still arguing. Poppy was standing at the bottom of the fire escape clutching a drooping fistful of yard mint and looking up puzzled. "Hey, what's going on?" she called up to me.

I guess I've never been happier to see anybody in my whole life. I put my finger to my lips and moved two steps down and whispered, "Get Tilford Jones! Hurry! You know, up on the second floor! Tell him to get Mr. Skeehan. He'll know who I mean!"

I figure city kids know an emergency when they see one because right off Poppy dropped the mint and headed around toward the front door. I knew I would be grateful to her forever.

I gathered my courage and climbed carefully back up the steps to where I could peek over Mrs. Potts's window ledge.

Now the man had hold of Mrs. Potts's wrist. "Don't try to fool me you can't remember where you hid that letter. I'm giving you five minutes and then — "

The letter! He must be talking about Mr. Skeehan's letter! So Mrs. Potts had it after all. What would the man do if she didn't give it to him? My mouth was cottony and my fingers ached where I was clutching the fire escape railing. Would he kill Mrs. Potts right there in front of my eyes? Oh, please hurry, Tilford, I prayed.

"Now!" The man yelled.

"I'll get it! I'll get it!" poor Mrs. Potts cried. Her hair was falling around her face and she looked awful.

The man let go of her. "And while you're at it," he demanded, "let that danged cat out of the closet. I'll fix those kids so they'll be too scared to talk!"

I felt like someone had zapped me with a ray gun. What did he mean? Did that man and Mrs. Potts have my cat locked up in a closet?

I took a step closer to the window as Mrs. Potts slowly crossed the room and opened a book lying on a table. The book looked like a Bible.

"I might have known," the man sneered.

I watched in wonder as Mrs. Potts took out a yellowed envelope. But while she was still holding the envelope, she opened a door beside the table.

Out ran a cat!

"Soon Gone!" I heard myself scream. Without even thinking I jumped through the open window. Quick as I got my feet under me I took out after Soon Gone. A shrill cry that must have come from

Mrs. Potts seemed to fill the room. The man reached down and grabbed Soon Gone, and I jumped onto his back.

Soon Gone likely clawed the man good because he spit out some terrible words and dropped her. Then he shook me off his back. I landed in a heap beside Soon Gone whose fur was standing on end all the way down her back. Her ears laid flat to her head. I scooped her up and held her close. The mean man with the earring was towering over me.

18

To my ever-lasting relief, I heard a sharp pounding on Mrs. Potts's door. Then I heard Mr. Skeehan yell, "Open up in the name of the law!"

The man and Mrs. Potts froze in place.

I saw my chance and took it. I grabbed Soon Gone closer and made a mad dash for the door, all the time expecting to feel the evil man's fingers clutch into my back. I made it to the door and turned the key. The door crashed open.

Mr. Skeehan was standing there holding up his night watchman's billy club. He was wearing a blue striped night shirt with a funny-looking cap hanging off to one side of his head. Hanging heavy from his nightshirt was his night watchman's badge. Behind him were Tilford and Poppy.

There was a pounding of feet on the steps and

from behind all of them Tilford's dad yelled, "What in the name of pink elephants is going on?"

Mr. Skeehan marched into the room and the others practically tumbled in behind him.

I yelled, "Mr. Skeehan! Mrs. Potts has your letter!"

Everyone looked at Mrs. Potts. The man with the earring stepped in front of her. "The kid's crazy," he said. "What is this? Breaking and entering my mother's apartment, that's what! I'll get the law on you — all of you."

Mother's apartment! I gasped. This awful man was poor Mrs. Potts's son!

"I *am* the law!" Mr. Skeehan shouted bravely. "I command you to return my property — now."

I was rightly proud of Mr. Skeehan. He didn't seem to be scared one mite. Even when the evil man gave him a shove.

"Out of my way, Grandpa." He sneered. "Scram kids." He brushed past Poppy, Tilford, and me and ran down the second floor steps before we could make a move.

"Shall I call the police, sir?" Tilford asked Mr. Skeehan.

"No!" Mr. Skeehan shouted. "I'll handle this."

"Please don't call the police," Mrs. Potts

119

begged. "I have the letter. It was all my fault."

By now the doorway to the hall was full of people. The commotion had brought Mr. Digsby and Miss Kate over to see what the goings on were all about. Even Miss Lizzie was slowly climbing the first flight of steps. I heard Tilford's dad trying to explain to everyone, "It's something about a letter. . . ."

Mrs. Potts handed the yellowed envelope to Mr. Skeehan. "I'm sorry, truly sorry," she said. "I owed my son Vincent some money," she explained sniffling a little. "I lost the money he inherited from his father. He was pushing me to get it somehow. It was my idea to steal your letter, Mr. Skeehan. I was going to sell it and pay Vincent back."

I looked at Mr. Skeehan who was looking inside the envelope as if making sure the letter was really there. He was blinking hard like he might be near to crying.

I hoisted Soon Gone higher in my arms and whispered to Tilford, "You think Mr. Peter Skeeter's okay?"

"Sure," Tilford said. "He's just excited."

Mrs. Potts was saying, "I talked Vincent into

pretending to be a delivery man to get inside your apartment. I knew Miss Lizzie would give him the key because I heard her tell the girl and her mother that it was hard for her to climb the steps anymore."

"But how did either one of you even know about my letter?" Mr. Skeehan asked gruffly. "And how did you know I kept it in my mother's old journal?"

"Everything was there in your own letter — the one to the President," Mrs. Potts admitted, looking around guiltily at all of us. "I saw the letter in the basket in the hall waiting for the postman to pick it up. When I first took it, I was only curious to find out why you, Mr. Skeehan, would be writing to the President of the United States. I meant to put the letter right back." Tears were streaming down her face.

"So the President didn't even get my letter," Mr. Skeehan said, looking happier. "I thought surely if he did, he would have answered it." Clasping his Lincoln letter to the front of his night shirt, he turned to leave. By now, his night cap was lying on the floor of Mrs. Potts's living room. The rest of us spread out into the hallway in front of him.

"Is that all?" Mrs. Potts called after Mr. Skeehan. "You aren't going to report me to the police or anything?"

"Why would *I* need the police?" Mr. Skeehan asked, swinging his night watchman's stick and winking at Tilford and me. "But I'm warning you now, Mrs. Potts, that it's a Federal offense to tamper with the United States Mail, and if I ever hear of you doing it again — "

Miss Lizzie and Miss Kate began telling Mr. Skeehan how glad they were he had his Lincoln letter back again. Even shy Mr. Digsby came over to shake his hand.

Though I hadn't noticed before, Mama had come home on the tail end of all this excitement. Tilford's dad was telling her what had happened as they walked up the wide stairway together.

Tilford, Poppy, and I went out to the front porch. Mr. Peter Skeeter's Confederate flag was waving in a strong breeze off oceanside. The three of us sat on the top step with me holding Soon Gone, and Poppy sitting in the middle.

19

For a while we all three sat there, not talking, just staring out at the huge live oaks dripping with their gray witch's hair.

After all the excitement poor Soon Gone seemed content to snooze on my lap. "What do you suppose that awful man was threatening to do to my cat?" I asked after I had told them what Mrs. Potts's son said about "fixing those snoopy kids" and about the note around Soon Gone's neck earlier.

Poppy smoothed Soon Gone's fur. "Gives you the shivers, doesn't it?"

Tilford said, "That man better not ever show up around here again or my dad — Say, Dorinda," he interrupted himself, "I guess I sort of need to say I'm sorry about the way I acted this morning."

"That's okay," I said quickly, "I knew you were just worried that your father — "

"Far as that goes," Tilford broke in, "my dad found out this morning he can get a loan to go to New York City for the — the tryouts for Clown College," he finished, looking belligerently at Poppy.

Poppy ducked her head and glanced sideways at Tilford. "Probably really *is* one," she sort of whispered.

"Thanks, Poppy," Tilford said softly, making one of his funny little bows.

Poppy smiled. I guessed maybe she was going to like staying at Winfield House after all.

"I'd better go up and see if Mama needs me," I said, getting up from the step.

Poppy stood up, too. "Guess I better go see about Miss Lizzie," she said.

Soon as I got inside our door, Mama said, "I declare, honey, it's a good thing your brothers will be gettin' home from their summer classes next week. By the time they have to leave again your school will be starting, and you won't be alone so much. When I think of you climbin' in that window. . . ." But I noticed right off that Mama didn't really look too upset.

124

I gave a silent little thank you to Tilford's dad for making the whole thing sound like it wasn't too terrible. "You don't need to worry," I explained to Mama. "Like I said, I know everyone in this big old house, and lots of them are my friends."

My forehead didn't even tickle. That's because it's true! I thought. Maybe not Mrs. Potts, but now that I know about her awful son, I can kind of see why she acts the way she does. And I even feel sorry for her.

That night in bed as I listened to the last night songs of the birds, and then the distant swamp songs of Creepin' Charlie, I thought about my dad. I thought about how always if you try to understand why someone does something, you forgive them. Just like Mrs. Potts, and with Poppy who is now my good friend. I thought, when I see my dad again I'll ask him about the swamps and about the coot and the hern and what their night sounds are. And I'll hear him callin' me Sisterbaby the way he used to.

I thought about school starting again. And about how it would be, walking to the end of the tabby lane with Tilford each morning to catch the school bus.

Would Poppy have to go back to New York then? If she did, I knew that, like Miss Lizzie, I would dream of the day when she would come back for good. The day when Winfield House would be filled with William's and Miss Lizzie's black angels. And Tilford and me, too, of course.